# SELENA (A) THIRUNIRAISELVY

ENNUM EZHUTHUM - NUMBER AND TEXT

KRITHIKA YEGNA

Made with ♥ on the Notion Press Platform
www.notionpress.com

To Appa...

You lead me

You are with me

You know I always need you, Appa.

How much ever I age, I would always be your, Pinchaali Pinchuli...

Dedicated to all my Gurus

# Contents

# Contents

# Foreword

Tamil is one of the most ancient languages. Tamil literature has been thought to include either descriptions of their land, or have been considered metaphorical poetry. Tamil texts have rarely been considered as coded.

The Tamil language has words that mean different things with reference to context. A term can mean opposites when read forward and backwards. And this led to attempting the decoding of the text, that has stayed popular for over 2000 years through the journey of ThirunirаiSelvy.

Thirunirai Selvy, is an ambitious girl with aspirations to explore the world and become a particle physicist. How destiny had other plans for her is what the series is all about.

She rediscovers, decodes the Thirukkural, and understands the true potential of an anthology of 7 worded couplets which have been thought of as lessons of life or mere poetry.

This book is also my journey as I attempt this medium of communication. And I am hopeful that many of the traditional practices that haven't been followed and are questioned and ridiculed just because the reasons and explanations were lost somewhere would find logical explanations through the story of ThiruniraiSelvy.

# Acknowledgements

This book wouldn't have been possible without my teachers. My humble respects to Ilangai Jeyaraj Ayya, Prof. K.L.Ramachandran(retd professor of Chemistry, DG Vaishnav College), Orissa Balu Ayya (Thenpulatharin Aiyai group), Karka Kasadara group, Voice of Valluvam group, Isaipuyal A.R.Rahman and all the guiding angels who have helped me.

My thanks are due to Gokulnath. I know you have put up with me the most in this journey. Thanks for believing in me and sponsoring my wild quests.

My children Aakash and Adhvyth, thanks for the patience and understanding, for the love both of you shower on me that makes me feel worthy.

My family, for the words of encouragement.

Special thanks to Chacku, and Peripa for help with Shorthand, my apathbandhavi Kavi, for editing the book.

My heartfelt thanks to my friends for the moral support.

Thanks to all my friends on various social media for the insightful conversations.

# Linguistic Conversions- Transliterations

Vowels

a- as in cap

aa- as in art

i-dip

ee- as in Deep

u- as in up

Oo-as in tool

e- as in step

a-tape

ai-as in tail

o- as in original

O-as in Ore

Ou-as in plough

Consonants

k-as in kite

Ch-as in chain

n-as in nine

N-as in palatal N

l-l as in angel

L-palatal L

CHAPTER ONE

# Siru Kai Alaaviya Koozh

"The world doesn't need a new particle collider", the headline that had got CERN worried and concerned about being shut down.

"We have had so many assignments that are completely outside our comfort zones the whole of last year. It is important to tell the world why our research is important and needs to be funded. The politicians and people would otherwise begin questioning about the money that is getting pumped into research and would ask about feeding the humans and about socio-economic priorities." Chaitanya's words echoed in Meena's head. She had been trying to organise a lot of things since then.

CERN was putting together a video which she thought would inspire children to choose a career at CERN. The young scientists at CERN were going to answer questions about Dark Matter.

Selena enthusiastically shared, "I am a software programmer taking care of detector technology for the ALICE experiment. This is part of the Muon tracker,"... Girls stop giggling, she said.

"Sorry... sorry, take 2," said Meena, nudging Ida to go to her console.

"CERN is home to several experiments that seek the particles that make up #darkmatter. These include experiments based at the Large Hadron Collider #LHC such as ATLAS and CMS, which have broken new ground in the search for dark-matter particles, and non-LHC experiments such as CAST and NA64, which too have added new knowledge about the properties of these hypothetical particles." typed out Selena.

"Meena, keep me out of the video. You know I prefer to be behind the scenes. Here, the YouTube description content is ready. Check that." said Selena

Meena said, 'alright, alright... you say the introduction about yourself again. I'll use it for something else. Maybe for some conference background filler videos."

Selena repeated what she had said earlier and then added, “I was looking for a role model like myself who was young and ambitious, and I hope the next generation draws inspiration from me.”

CERN had about 10,000 scientists and the covid pandemic had shut down CERN for the public. The scientists were already mentally stressed about their schedules and the open days were one chance to meet with an enthusiastic public. With that suspended, the girls had to plan something different to spread some cheer.

Selena was the most unenthusiastic about the idea since she had two things on her plate. It was a relief for her that as soon as she got into the campus, the campus shut. She had already made good progress in her secret research. But didn't know enough about its potential, or if this was a big deal at all. For now, she considered it as one of her decoding games she used to play with her cousin.

Selena was replaying the whole shoot in her mind as she sat on the couch at her cousin Dweepa's place in Geneva, Switzerland. Dweepa is Selena's paternal cousin. Her dad's sister's daughter. In fact, her only cousin. Dweepa's parents live in the US. Her husband is in the Merchant Navy.

Selena hated non-academic things like photo or video shoots. As a true software professional, she liked to be the behind-the-scenes/screen person. She considered Stephen Hawking as her Demi god and wanted to get to CERN even though she got a campus placement at the top MNCs immediately after her Bachelor of Engineering degree at Anna University. She was a University rank holder.

“SiNa, can I make you a sandwich for dinner?” asked Dweepa, calling her by the secret pet name. “Tini darling,” called Selena, using her pet name, “regardless of how I try to be the NRI that I have always dreamed of becoming, my Indian tongue doesn't let me be so. Is there some *dosai* batter?”

Dweepa said, “oh oh! I ran out of it just today, baby. And by the way, if you call me TiNi, that would make my birthday impossible, won't it?” She asked with a naughty smile.

“Okay... I won't mess it...” said Selena and added, “am amazed at our pet names you came up with so long ago...”

“SiNa, because I was born on 14 November, Silicon -Si Element 14 and sodium-Na, eleventh Element, since November is the 11$^{th}$ month' and 'Titanium-Ti, Element 22 and Na for 22$^{nd}$ November which is mine.” completed Dweepa, as she continued to feed her 6-month-old baby, some porridge.

Dweepa brought the Sandwich and handed it to Selena, who was trying hard to eat it without comparing it with the crispy dosai that her mom and Dweepa usually made.

"Aaki dolly... baby dolly... Why are you squishing that '*koozh*' darling? Look at yourself!" said Dweepa as she fondly took her babbling baby's bowl of porridge away.

Aakash smeared Dweepa's face with the porridge and Dweepa licked the drop that was at the edge of her lips. After cleaning the mess, Dweepa sat down with her bowl of soup. "That's dinner. I am on the diet that Yegna mami suggested for post pregnancy weight loss. Seriously, Yegna mami should have had a career. She made sure you and Sandy flourished and stayed at home. Can't imagine our generation taking such decisions, right?" she said

"The *koozh* tastes sweeter after my '*cheeni*' (meaning sugar, a fond expression she had for every baby) plays with it, you know," said Dweepa.

Selena sat up suddenly. She quickly took out and noted down something immediately in her notepad. She wanted to discuss it with Dweepa since they both have been partners in every crime since childhood. But Dweepa had to put the baby to sleep. So, Selena thought this could wait till the next morning.

Selena was tired after the shoot with all the moving around for the right spot, retakes, etc. She was a typical 2K kid, an Indian with a foreign dream.

She had changed her name, Thiruniraiselvy, to Selena. But, she wasn't the Instagram crazy, social media person. She loved her job and wanted to be a Nobel laureate someday.

Renuka athai, Dweepa's gynaecologist mom, was also an artist. Two of her paintings were in the room, that Selena went to sleep in. She recollected seeing them as photos. Looking at them as canvases was a unique experience. One had a woman making flower strings, but it depicted DNA being strung by her into chromosomes.

The other painting was of Naga devathas (snake gods). This was new. And she told herself that she would ask athai at a later point. Selena slept as soon as she hit the bed.

CHAPTER TWO

# SiNa and TiNa

"Selvi.. Sandy... how long will you guys take to get ready to school!" shouted, Yegna Lakshmi. "If you don't go now, Appa can't drop you and then you will have to take the bus," threatened Yegna Lakshmi.

It was Thiruniraiselvy's 3rd School. Her dad Anandan worked at the Ahmedabad Customs and Central Excise Department and was head of Air Cargo Customs division there. He was an IRS officer.

With every transfer they moved to a new state which spoke a new language. Thiruniraiselvy and Sandy therefore studied in the CBSE curriculum and both of them had Hindi as their second language and Sanskrit as their third language at school.

Tamil was only in their names, and they spoke Tamil at home. They had no other connection with their Native land.

Yegna Lakshmi was an enterprising woman. She adapted to every State with such poise and grace and within a month, could bargain at the local market like a localite.

Yegna graduated from Women's Christian College, Chennai and completed a master's degree in Nutrition and Dietetics from Ethiraj College, Chennai. She had been such a bright student but after marriage, since Anandan had a transferable job, she was a homemaker, and a small-time caterer.

She undertook small party orders.With her robust communication skills, she learnt not just languages but many dishes from every cuisine.

Anandan dropped them at school on his way, every day. The children were extremely studious, just like him. So, he had absolutely nothing to worry about. His issue was 'his' Hindi. He could never get himself to speak it and the moment he opened his mouth; the kids would burst out laughing.

He instructed the driver, "*wus Gate u ke paasu naghi rokuna, thoda aage jawke rokuna*' meaning don't stop right in front of the gate, please go a few paces ahead and stop."

The South-Indian-accented Hindi of Anandan made the driver giggle and he said, "*Ji saabji.*"

"Selvy *thangam, thambiya nalla paathukkada, pudhu school la*! Selvy darling, take care of your brother dear, it's a new school right," he said as always, whenever they moved to a new city.

"Thiruni-rai-sale-vy" called out the teacher with a heavy Gujarati accent. She confirmed if she called her name correctly and Selvy said, "madam, you can call me Selena." The teacher was visibly relieved.

Thiruniraiselvy introduced herself to everyone as Selena. It was only the records and documents that had her true Tamil name. She thought to herself. Thank God I chose the name for Sandy. Nobody would bully him.

Sandy came running during the recess, crying. He sobbed and said in a muffled voice "Why *Akka*, why did you name me Sandy? look.. they all threw sand on me and shouted,

"*Kem cho*, How are you? He is Sandy....Who is he?.. He is Sandy..."

Selvy /Selena was furious, but before she could pick up a fight, the teacher had come back, and Sandy had to rush back to his class.

Selena was like her dad. Not too social or street smart. She was a hardworking academic. Her favourite subject was always science.

She made a new friend Kiran, who started the conversation. She was a witty girl.

Selvy secretly liked chemistry. Selvy asked her what '*che*' meant in Gujarati. Kiran said "are/is."

"*Che Mystery che. Kem che*, mystery *Che...*" She laughed at her pathetic joke to herself and was waiting to get back home so that she could discuss it with her mom.

Yegna took an auto to bring the children home. As soon as they reached home, Sandy called his chiththi, his maternal aunt, his confidante, on the phone and cried a lot about the bullying he faced.

Anandavalli chiththi was Yegnalakshmi's only sister. She was a spinster who worked as a government school science teacher at Aralvaimozhi, Tamilnadu.

She suggested he could change his name if he wished, just like Selvy made it Selena.

Sandy was excited. He said he wanted to call himself something that sounded Tamil. He was the exact opposite of Selena.

She wanted to go abroad. She was their paternal aunt's (athai) pet. Selvy's role model was Dweepa.

Selvy took the receiver from Sandy, who was now much more cheerful since chiththi had pacified him with a lot of riddles he could use on his friends the next day and handle his bullies. Anandavalli chiththi was an expert at riddles. She was an amicable, chilled out, jovial school teacher.

"Selvy thangam," chiththi, called fondly and enquired about her day at school. Selvy shared her PJ (Pathetic joke) and chiththi laughed a lot and then ended the call after some sweet nothings.

"Look at this letter, Selena," called Yegna Lakshmi. It was from Dweepa. And it was already open. Selena was fuming at the sight of it.

Yegna then said as she was kneading the dough for the order she had got from a neighbour, a senior citizen couple. "Hey what are you girls up to? I couldn't make head or tail of it."

Selena felt relieved that Yegna could not read it and sat with her code key. They exchanged secret coded letters. Every vacation, they would decide their monthly codes and the letters would be based on those. This month's key was the easiest. It was a mirror image, letter wise and word wise.

So every word was in reverse and written in alphabetically mirrored letters. Though the content of the letter would be about silly things like the blooming of the rose plant or the exam scores of each other, it was their secret. Only theirs. Just like the secret pet names, SiNa(Dweepa) and TiNa(Selena).

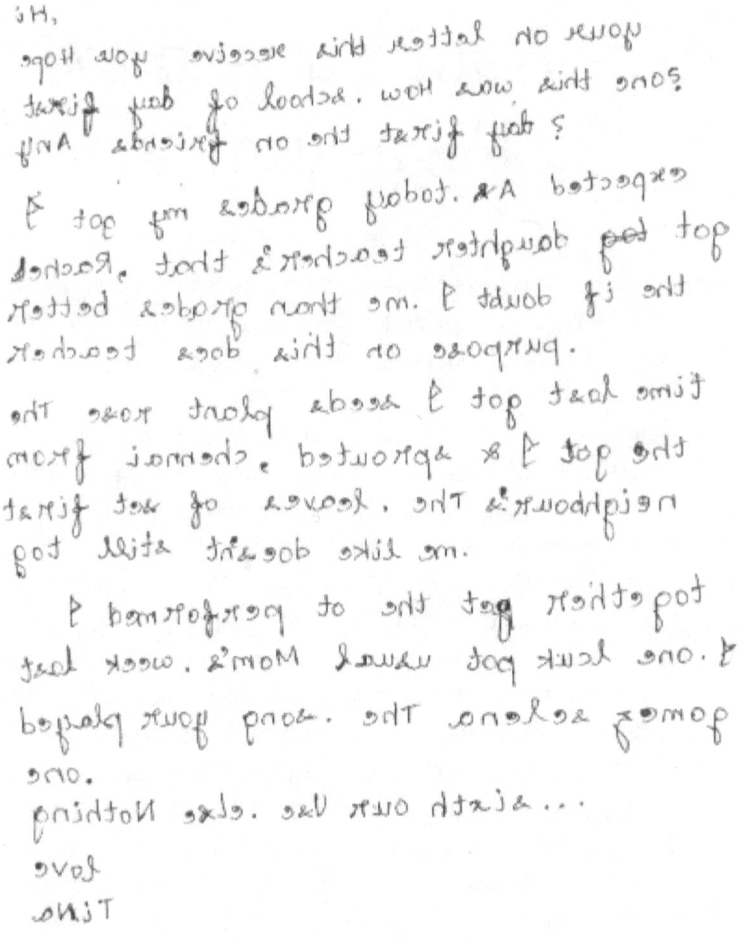

Hi,

Hope you receive this letter on your
first day of school. How was this one?
Any friends on the first day?

I got my grades today. As expected
Rachel, that teacher's daughter got top
better grades than me. I doubt if the
teacher does this on purpose.

The rose plant seeds I got last time
from Chennai, sprouted & I got the
first set of leaves. The neighbour's
dog still doesn't like me.

I performed at the get together
last week. Mom's usual pot luck one. I
played your song. The Selena Gomez
one.

Nothing else. Use our sixth...

Love

Tino

Enter Caption

CHAPTER THREE

# The Natarajar and the Ragasiyam

Thiruniraiselvy took out her precious letters which she had preserved since her school days. She always prided herself on being that agent who could decode anything. She had in fact self-published her first book, which she co-authored with her cousin.

But Thirukkural wasn't that easy a code. Mainly because she hadn't learnt Tamil formally. She put in an entire year's effort, a month to learn the Tamil script, and then a couple of months more to read from Parimel Azhagar's explanations, M. Karunanidhi's and Solomon Papaih's books.

She had made her own notes and had about 50 pages for each Adhigaram. In fact, she had recently discovered that Solomon Papiah wasn't a witty judge of a debate show that her dad watched every Pongal, but he was a Professor of Tamil, and the author of the easy guide for Thirukkural.

She could hardly concentrate on her job with all the research she was doing. She had established connections with just 7 Adhigarams and was still far away from getting fully convinced about the Thirukkural's potential.

She put the papers back as she heard her boss calling out her name. Thiruniraiselvy had forgotten the deadline again. It was her turn at the journal club. She had to think of some other excuse or ask her lab bestie Meena for a swap.

As if the universe conspired to help her, Lenka came running to her and asked if they could swap their sessions, since she was planning to go out on a date with the new senior scientist who had joined last month.

Selvy was more than happy. She then spoke to her boss and let her know about the change.

The talk was a complete OHP for her, Overhead projection. Not one word got into Selvy's head. She badly needed her caffeine break. Though it could never be her South Indian filter coffee, she needed something to calm her mind. After the coffee, she went straight to the Natarajar statue again. It has now become her daily ritual. She had to look at Natarajar, the presiding deity of Chidambaram, the *Aakasha sthalam,* the temple honouring the 'space'.

Shaivites, the worshippers of Lord Shiva, had 5 temples which represent the five elements of nature. It blew her mind to know that these temples were all on different locations latitudinally, but on the 79 degree longitude. The Aakasha, or space as one of the five elements, has a lot of reverence. There may be various reasons for CERN to bring the statue of Natarajar. But for Selvy, it was acting as that medium through which she was trying to communicate with the ancient scholars.

She went back to her desk, browsing through the letters. She was trying to check all those letters that had to do with cracking numbers. As she searched, she heard her *chiththi*'s voice saying '*Ennum ezhuththum Kann ena thagum*' meaning Numbers and text are to be revered as our eyes.

CHAPTER FOUR

# Kuzhal inidhu Yaazh inidhu - The musical painting

Geneva, February 2022

Selvy had the day off and spent the whole day at Dweepa's place. But Dweepa's husband had come home, and she didn't want to be the babysitter as the couple met after a long time.

She was forced to accompany Lenka, Meena, and Lenka's boyfriend for lunch. Meena wanted company.

Meena Ahir Yadav was from Patna. Selvy had spent two years in Patna, Bihar and thus they became besties very quickly. They had planned to tour the Museum at Geneva. After a week of not being able to move out of the console, they wanted to walk and lubricate their joints.

Meena had faced a lot of stares from some of her Indian friends. She faced some discrimination as a Bihari and was bullied asking if her father was a cowherd. She loved exploring heritage and was proud of her land being the Oxford of the Gupta Period, with Nalanda University and the great Chandragupta Maurya's capital city, Pataliputra. Meena felt horrible at the state her State was in now. She discussed with Selvy about secret societies of the world, which could have been conspirators who made sure no one had pride for the wealth they had under their feet and were lured by marketed 'Fashion' be it in clothes, language, food or even marriage. "They mocked polygamy but 'living in' relationship was trendy," she commented as they walked. At the entrance of the museum they saw a couple who had clearly come there to get cozy and not to look at the exhibits. They both looked at each other and smiled.

While Selvy was confused with whatever Meena talked about, as in her heart she was a non-resident foreigner till she was in India. She had no attachment to her roots or was least patriotic. She looked at the exhibits with a lot of awe. Meena was scanning through exhibits to find clues which could help her prove Europeans were mere traders and the treasures displayed were owned by Kings of the lands they travelled to.

Both saw the museum at their own paces and agreed to meet at the entrance at 4 PM. Selvy had finished seeing the exhibits sooner since she wasn't a history person at all. She believed in technology and didn't want to live in the past. She saw a small crowd outside the museum where artists were drawing portraits of people 'on the spot'.

There was a French artist who was doing something unique. Few people were near him. She went closer to watch. He had asked them to name their favourite song, and made small tile abstracts based on the song. This process was intriguing and she wanted to get one for her song choice. She chose 'Revival' by Selena Gomez. She thought to herself, I am part of a quest to revive, and my favourite artist also releases a song named 'Revival'

The artist noted down the song and heard it after she sent it to him on Bluetooth. He jotted down the musical notes of the song effortlessly and did something more. He assigned colours to the notes and made an abstract painting. It extremely impressed her. She couldn't imagine they could combine two such things as music and fine art this way.

After the wonderful trip, both Meena and Selvy were exhausted, and they reached their rooms so tired that they didn't even have energy to have dinner they had bought on their way from the regular chain that's all around the world.

Selvy thought of eating that for breakfast the next day and, after carefully placing the painting on her table, went to bed. She struggled to sleep. She kept staring at the painting and dozed off without realising when.

She had a strange dream. The colours of the painting were dancing like a kaleidoscope to the tune of 'revival', the patterns slowly aligned into a spectrum. It wasn't a rainbow. It was a 'Spectrum', like a line spectrum of some element. She had images of the man decoding the spectrum back to musical notes and the notes were now being played by Anandavalli chiththi on the Veenai. The song wasn't a cheerful song. But she couldn't get the tune out of her head. She heard baby Aakash molly coddling in the same tune. But Dweepa was listening to Aakash as if he was singing at a Carnatic Music concert.

Selvy woke up profusely, sweating. She looked. It was 4:32 AM. She wondered how, after she had begun the quest with Thirukkural, she was constantly seeing these Tesla numbers 3,6 and 9.

432 had significance as the natural pitch to which musical instruments should be tuned to, for them to work as healing agents. She was a hardcore music buff. 4+3+2 made 9. The number that controls all numbers. She recalled the conversation with her Paati's neighbours. She thought she would ask them when she went to Chennai.

The scientist Nikola Tesla had observed that the biological activity was in the pattern of doubling.

Number 1 doubles to 2, then 4, 8, 16.

If we add the two-digit numbers and keep them as single digits, then the sequence would be,1, 2, 4, 8, 7(1+6), 5(3+2), 1(6+4), 2(1+2+8), ... 1, 2, 4, 8, 7, 5 and so on.

Among the numbers from 0 through 9, the numbers that don't occur in this sequence are 3, 6 and 9. The number 6 occurs by doubling 3.

But 9 doesn't feature in any of this. 9 can only be obtained with multiples of 9. The multiplication table would have 1, 18, 27, 36, 45, and so on. 3, 6 and 9 are the Tesla numbers.

She didn't want to forget anything she saw or heard. She jotted everything along with the time. Even the tune. She, in fact, hummed it and recorded it on her mobile. She was getting more and more curious about all these but her education system, which was completely based on Mc Caulay's, constantly pulled her back, saying, 'Where is the documented evidence? How can you believe in things like intuition or angel numbers?' She told herself that she would wait for her to at least get to *Adhigaram* 19. If it still made sense, she would meet the research scholar of *Paati*, Thoothukudi Jeyaraman.

CHAPTER FIVE

# One year ago- The "VeLi"

ThiruniraiSelvy received the mail she was waiting for the whole day. It was her letter of appointment and offer for the job that was her 15+ year dream.

She wanted to be a scientist even as a 5-year-old. That was her first costume for the Fancy dress competition. Now it would soon be reality.

She had used her vacations throughout her BE to equip herself with all the skills she could think of. Anna University and University of Madras, Chennai, share the campus. Anna university students were the cream of the society. They had the best scores among 10 lakh aspirants. The students had the advantage of sharing the campus with research scholars and masters' students of the University of Madras. Their campus was also opposite the IIT, Madras. They had friends from all these institutions who met frequently at the bus stop.

ThiruniraiSelvy was reluctant to socialise, but she was exceptionally sharp. Her friends thought interacting with other campuses wasn't a great idea, since they felt they were the best. Students at Madras University, according to them, studied in rural colleges and then joined there for Masters.

But since Selvy grew up in all States of India, she was far more respectful. All that mattered to her was the gain of knowledge. She spent her time in the Nuclear Physics department or the Theoretical Physics department, or the department of Crystallography and Biophysics, of the University of Madras, meeting the Ph. D scholar *annas* and *akkas* there. The lab culture in the Universities in Tamil Nadu was to refer to seniors as elder brother or sister.

She was part of the astronomy club. She applied for summer research fellowships and went to different labs each year during the vacations.

It was no surprise to anyone in her family that she landed at CERN.

After being such a non-resident foreigner in India, the Natarajar struck her at CERN. Selvy couldn't fake it when she felt she knew nothing about the Natarajar statue or its spiritual significance.

She didn't know what cosmic dance was. She had known that there was a Natarajar statue there, but all that she was browsing about were other things. It was her friends who made her feel important as a person who hailed from the land the statue came from. She felt like the 'chosen one'.

Her parents were not too religious. Yegna believed '*makkal thonde magesan thondu*' meaning service to fellow humans was worship of the divine. Her dad was a writer after he came back from work. He wrote books about taxation laws, or researched the various aspects of the latest budget, or would take classes in the local IAS coaching centre whichever city they transferred him to.

Selvy called her *chiththi*, someone whom she had never taken seriously in life earlier. To Selvy, Anandavalli *chiththi* was a person filled with love, but was an unambitious, unsuccessful school teacher who worked at a village government school. She was someone who used to just talk about Tamil pride. She used to think, a person who hasn't pursued studies when she had the opportunity to excel, and has been serving in a school, wouldn't be a able to motivate the students to achieve more. She wondered how these young minds could be demotivated at someone like her.

Selvy didn't believe in instincts or intuition, but today, it was as if Natarajar had asked Selvy to call Anandavalli.

"Selvy... *thangam... sollu da...* CERN *poitiya*? Have you reached CERN?" asked Anandavalli.

Before Selvy responded, chiththi read the pause. She asked, "*Natarajar silai paathu merandutiya?* Are you stunned looking at the statue?" Selvy was speechless. "How did *Chiththi* know!" she thought.

The same instinct that asked her to call *chiththi* made her wonder if *chiththi* wasn't as innocent or ignorant as Selvy thought. She was getting emotional, and didn't understand why.

Anandavalli said, "It is time for you to visit us dear. When you find time, come home to Aral. It is time for 'you' now... It is high time..."

Anandavalli's words were disturbing. Selvy browsed that whole day about Chidambaram, Natarajar, the cosmic dance, Manikkavasagar, etc. She also vowed to learn to read and write Tamil.

She felt that '*Chidambara ragasiyam*', the secret of Chidambaram, was waiting for her to decode.

She kept repeating the sentence '*Chidambara ragasiyam verondrum illai, adhu veliyil ulladhu*' which she heard on a YouTube video. Which would translate straight away to mean the secret of Chidambaram is outside.

She thought deeper and deeper, and her phone rang. It was Yegna, her mom. “Amma, you called at such a crucial time,” said Selvy unenthusiastically.

When Yegna asked, “Selena *kutty, enna da*! I hope you aren't missing home already,” she asked. She had the mother's instinct and asked Selena what was bothering her but clarified that it was just a routine call from her end.

Selvy shared her puzzling sentence, ‘*Chidambara ragasiyam verondrum illai, adhu veliyil ulladhu*’, with her mom. Yegna was a born linguist. She explained how the Tamil language had amazing words.

She said, “*keLvi* is a word that means,” and Selvy said... “Question.”

Yegna said, “yes. It also means the ability to hear. Or learn through listening. By asking a (*KeLvi*) question, what you develop is knowledge through listening. Asking is also *keLvi,* receiving the answer was also through *KeLvi,* she explained. Similarly, ‘*VeLi* in Tamil does not just mean ‘outside’. It means space. That includes both the outer space and the space between. It is that space where everything happens, like the formless stage for a play to be performed.”

Yegna dumbfounded Selvy. It suddenly struck her so hard that she disconnected the call and bent down, tears rolling down her cheeks.

She had just completed writing the program where she had considered the gravitational force field and the gluons that were bothering her.

She had been considering particles without the force field and with the force field. She knew the force field was like that fabric on which the particles were suspended. And that space wasn't representing a complete lack of something, that's vacuum, but something that decided how far or near each particle is and how the vibration of one would affect the other.

*Amma* explained it effortlessly, ‘formless stage’. “It took me 5 slogging years to understand particle physics.” she thought to herself. Selvy felt ashamed about her attitude towards her mother and her native language. She was waiting for the six-monthly break she had informed her boss about. She had too many things noted down in her Notepad that awaited clarification from her chiththi. This trip wasn't because of homesickness. It was Homeland sensitization and the ‘native tongue sting’.

CHAPTER SIX

# Ennum Ezhuthum

After World War II, European scientific research was significantly impacted. Some French, Dutch, and Italian scientists came up with a resolution in the United Nations and decided to establish a research facility in one of the European countries. This research facility was to be common for world nations, and European countries agreed that no research related to war technologies or anything that could lead to destruction would take place there. CERN, located in Geneva, Switzerland. This place has been in existence since then. It has recently been opened to the public for viewing. Places like 'Cube of Science Innovation' and 'Idea Square' have been built in a way that attracts visitors with their monumental architecture. Various categories of visitors, such as school students, individuals, and families, can register via the website and visit in person. These sites were empty this year. If it weren't for the COVID infection, they would have been overflowing with crowds of the general public. While there was indeed such commotion on the surface, the actual research facility of CERN was situated beneath these viewing sites, located several meters underground.

Meena urged Selvy to accompany her to the lowest point at -56 m, below the ground where the beam line would be functional soon.

Selvy was terrified of heights, depth, and water. As she went down, her heart was beating faster, she imagined 32 people of her height stacked one above another to recall how deep down they were. She felt dizzy and told Meena she had to get back to the console.

The trip down made her sick and the lack of sleep had also tampered with her digestion. The main reason being, she had to survive on burgers, cheese sandwiches, Pizzas every day since it was difficult to find healthier options in the odd times that she could eat. She threw up 7 times and Meena started to worry. She accompanied Selvy to her room and asked her to catch up on some sleep. She promised to get her South Indian food for dinner.

Selvy was dreaming again. *Ennum Ezhuthum Kann ena thagum*. She had that being repeated with the images of the stacks of Selvy underground. They multiplied and arranged themselves into a table. She saw that the Selvys in the tabular arrangement were holding boards with numbers written on them. The numbers ran from 1 to 132. There was a Selvy on a separate box above the table with three hoola hoops moving around like the symbol for an atom. She was also holding a shield with three circles, two down and one up. The circles below were larger than the one above. The numbered Selvys zoomed out now. She felt the Table was too familiar. It had the Selvy's 119-132 standing in a separate row. She had the image of a lotus with petals opening to a circle with 1, with the shield. One circle had an arrow upwards. The two below had arrows pointing downwards, suddenly... Thor's hammer hit the whole thing, shattering the blocks of the table and the petals of the flower... she woke up with a bad headache... It was the door.

Meena brought her *dosai* and *uthappam*. She felt so relieved to eat something she considered human food. But she was so hungry that she didn't feel full at all. She had to trouble Meena again, to get her some strawberry flavoured Greek yogurt, the closest to sweet lassi, that she said she had in her room. She hoped yogurt would soothe her regurgitation.

Selvy hadn't realised how long she had slept. She was, in fact, wondering why Meena hadn't got her some rice. Meena then said it was the next morning and that the restaurant only served breakfast that early. Selvy felt embarrassed.

She began writing about her dream. She tried to draw the table that she saw in her dream, sipping some water. Selvy had been sharing her research with Meena since she was a heritage lover. Meena saw the shield and the hoola hoop and asked, "is that the neutron dear?" Selvy almost spit out the water.

Meena said "the shield had two down quarks and an up quark. And the 14 numbers after 118!!! Means the F, right?" Selvy hugged her tight and said... "You are my best friend *re*." So that's where it is in Thirukkural, she told herself and took out Valli *chiththi*'s papers and looked up to see the kurals under the first chapter.

She understood what Anandavalli *Chiththi* had meant. *Ennum ezhuthum kann ena thagum. Ennum* can mean number or act of thinking. *Ezhuthum* is a text. *Kann ena thagum*. Are to be revered like one's eyes. Or they are 'the eyes' through which you should seek. So, the code was, seek with the number, after you align, seek through the text.

She had cracked the number now. She felt more hopeful. She suddenly remembered the yellow pouch that her Paati gave her. It had the exact thing inscribed. A line drawing of a girl with hoops and a shield with 3 circles.

She began pursuing her quest with more trust. She felt initially that she needed to wait until 19 *Adhigarams*. But she felt convinced now that there was indeed something worthwhile in the pursuit. She had deciphered the single box and had given little thought, but now the neutron seemed like a perfect fit. The one that has all the elementary particles necessary. She also could not believe that she got his on 7$^{th}$ January, and that she had just completed cracking *adhigaram* 7. Again, a number that has Kural connections. 1+3+3=7, Kural meter has 7 words. Number 7 had so much to do with Thirukkural. She noted down that too. She was just left with one notepad, and made a mental note in her shopping list

CHAPTER SEVEN

# Aralvaimozhi

Selvy had asked Yegna to come to Aralvaimozhi. A beautiful village near the Podigai mountains. The range wasn't as tall as the Himalayas, not even the Western ghats. But had a lot of significance for Tamils. The father of Tamil language, Sage Agathiyar, is believed to have been born in this region of Tamilnadu.

Yegna had to travel from New Delhi to where Anandan was posted. She and Sandy flew to Trivandrum, where she joined Selvy, who had reached the airport from Switzerland. They took the Anantapuri express from Trivandrum to reach Aralvaimozhi, aramboly as called by malayalees.

Sandy was growing to be a young man. "Sandy, how have you become so quiet?" asked Selvy.

Sandy said with a straight face. "Call me Sendhan! I have changed my name in the government gazettes too." he spoke with his new cracked adolescent voice. His baby voice had gone. It felt strange and she chuckled. She thought of the little boy who had been so dependent on his akka. At the same time, she felt guilty of how long it had been since she had spoken to her younger brother, with the compassion she had years ago. After her tenth grade, she had stayed at her grandmother's house in Chennai. After that, even during the summer vacations of her undergraduate studies, she had continued to study without wasting time. She had somehow become selfish, she thought. She had lost her darling brother somewhere.

Selvi was aware of how much Sandy loathed his meaningless name and how intense his desire was to change it. Sandy once told her, 'Sand, is the type of soil that doesn't bind to anything. That name doesn't suit my character at all.'"

He spoke so rudely that she could literally read the number of beeps that were supposed to be muted. The untold expressions showed the cuss words he wanted to howl at her for choosing a meaning-less name.

'*Chiththi* gave me this name. Sendhan', he said.

Even though Selvy was getting curious about the language, she wasn't the Tamil fanatic that Sandy, sorry Sendhan, had become.

She was a scientist, and she needed documented evidence for anything and everything. The stories of India were meaningless to her. Ramayanam was one epic she hated. She could never call a man who doubted his pregnant wife and let her go to a forest as even a 'human being with values', leave alone considering him a hero. She couldn't visit temples without a thousand questions bombarding her head.

But Sendhan had transformed. The jallikaatu protests of 2016 had created such an impact upon him, he began saying "*#munnorgal muttalgal alla*!" meaning 'ancestors were not fools', for everything.

Yegna, sensing the tension between the two, called out to Selena and said, "*Athai* called to say that Dweepa delivered a baby boy," just to lighten the mood.

"I know" said Selvy, with a look that said, "*Amma*, she's my 'bum-chum' won't I be the first one to know when Dweepa delivered a baby?"

Within minutes of the mention of Dweepa's name, she pinged Selvy on WhatsApp. "Tell me what I should name the baby... Soon... I have to register the name before getting discharged." Without a second's delay, Selvy typed, "AAKASH"

Dweepa immediately understood why she suggested this name. She replied, "*Chidambara ragasiyam 'Veliyil'*!!!"

Aralvaimozhi welcomed the trio. She couldn't recall how it used to look before, but, she was stunned to see the windmills. The village looked beautiful with greenery and hills all around. It surprised her at how humid it was. The wind was blowing away the heat, yet it was exceptionally warm, probably because she had got there directly from CERN, Switzerland.

Anandavalli had been waiting to receive them. "Sendhan..." she squeaked and gave him her fond hug.

"Selvy Selena, *vaa daa*, welcome dear," she said with lesser enthusiasm.

Yegna had brought two suitcases for a week's stay. Selvy knew one was full of stuff that would be distributed, and then refilled with *vathal*(sun dried-ready to fry snacks), *appalam*, *puli* (tamarind), *marachekku*(wood-cold pressed) oil, etc.

"*Chiththi*, have you changed your car?" asked Sendhan. Anandavalli said, "no dear, it is the same maruti swift desire that you saw last time."

They reached home and Selvy felt the same icy stare from her grandmother as ever. Yegna urged Selvy and Sendhan to take grandmother's blessings.

She called out Thiruniraiselvy, "*va daa, paati kitta aseervadham vaangikko*, Take her blessings."

Sendhan had already prostrated at the feet of the retired Tamil Professor, Bala. When Selvy was about to bend, Bala walked away, saying, "*pal varisayila paadhi.... pulla vayithulerndhu vandhiduchu...kettu pogala... kannu, kaadhu, mookilla, kai, kaalu, naakila...*"

Selvy was confused, as always. Sendhan too. Anandavalli translated the riddle for them, saying

"*Pal varisaiyila paadhi*- Half of the number of teeth- 16

*Pulla vayithulerndhu vandudichu*- 'Baby 'Delivered- or *Petru* (blessed with)

*Kettu pogala* - it is not spoilt, means it is good- *nalla...*

*Kannu kaadhu, mookilla*

*Kai kaalu, naakilla*- eyes are two, two ears, not the nose, two arms, legs two, not the tongue -"

Sendhan completed the blessing... "16 *Petru nalla iru,* meaning stay richly blessed with 16 kinds of prosperous things."

For the first time, the meaningless squiggles all over the house, the Thirukkural charts on the walls of paati's house made sense.

She read "*KoLil poriyil guNamilave enguNathaan thaaLai vaNangaa thalai,*" written below the portrait of Valluvar that chiththi had painted. It was an unusual painting. Not the one in which they drew him as the meditating saint. This looked like a scientist.

She was slowly getting more curious about *chiththi* as a person. Just like she felt, Thirukkural and Valluvar were completely mysterious. *Chiththi* and *Paati* were mysteries to solve, too.

Grandma's house was the traditional Tamil home. It was beautifully structured with a courtyard in the center, and rooms surrounding it. The windows and doors were designed to let in air and light to every corner of the house. Unlike the modern homes and the white rooms in Switzerland she had lived in, this house had young green walls, that too the walls had acrylic water proof emulsion paint with a darker shade of green on the lower part of the wall and lighter green from about the middle till the ceiling.

It had unique teak wood windows and doors. Though switches were old, they were still in good condition, the house was well-maintained despite its age.

To enter the house, one had to climb three steps at the entrance. There were small platforms for sitting on either side of the stairs. In one corner of the platform, a pot filled with water sat atop a mound of sand, ready to quench the thirst of passersby. In the entrance, a small jar hung from the roof, filled with rice and grains for the birds. Two bowls were set up for the street dogs: one filled with water and the other containing a portion of the day's leftovers. On the northern side of the house, there was a swing. Doors were present in all directions, except for the main entrance door, the other doors had been split into two. The lower halves of the doors alone could be latched. This ensured animals couldn't come in, and children couldn't crawl away, as Mom would say.

There was also a beautiful natural garden with an grinding stone, a pounding stone, a pot for hot water, and numerous trees. This garden was wonderfully wild and lush, rather than being neatly manicured. It hosted various plants like banana trees, coconut palms, mango trees, neem trees, jasmine, hibiscus, mallow species, mandara (a flowering plant), tulsi (holy basil), guava, snake gourd, bitter gourd, and ivy gourd among others. There was also a well. The bathing area and toilets were located on the outer side. Even now, Chiththi would say "I'm going to the backyard" instead of saying "I'm going to the toilet."

The house was decorated with solid wooden furniture. The Sofa in the living room, chairs, etc were made of teak wood. The bedrooms did not have cots. Only Paatti's had a cot which was set higher than those in the urban set ups. The other rooms had mattresses wrapped in a mat and were opened only when it was time to sleep. She recalled paatti saying the impressions of our body would be there on a bed after we wake up and it would call for demons to take not of our measurements and scare us. The bed in Paatti's room was made after much convincing after her health had deteriorated.

On the terrace, there were sheets of Plastic on which many things were left for Sundrying. There were rice crisps, chillies, coriander seeds, etc. Selena understood that these were for making sambar powder which Yegna would pack when she leaves. The stairs were also made entirely of wood. There was an easy chair on the Southern side of the main hall. This was the one thatha used every morning when he read the newspaper, while sipping his filter coffee. There was a rocking chair for Paatti. It was her ritual to sit on it with closed eyes as Tamil music, Thevaaram etc were played on a casette player, every morning after she took bath.

The floor was a cement floor polished with 'red oxide,' shining brightly and well-maintained in eventhough it was black, this type of flooring was called 'red oxide'. The kitchen was a blend of modern and traditional styles. It had a platform resembling a modular kitchen, but the utensils were old yet well-kept. Items like wooden ladles, brass pots, and clay dishes were neatly washed and organized. Valli Chithi was chopping vegetables on a traditional cutting board.

"The cooking is done, dear! I'm cutting some green mangoes and adding salt and chili," Chithi said.

"I'm not hungry, Chithi. I hadn't been here for a long time, that's why I wanted to look around and enjoy," Selina replied.

The clay tiled roof of the kitchen had a few glass tiles, which made sure the kitchen was well lit during the day.

"I hope you didnt't go to my room! I just left my clothes lying around. It's all done now, dear. Come, let's go there and continue chatting," Chithi suggested.

Chithi's room was very beautiful. Her veena was in one corner, and her desk was on the other side, beautifully organized with neatly stacked papers. There was a large pile of new books on physics in the corner, including Russian, Japanese, and German titles. In another corner were materials for Chithi's paintings. Chithi kept her sarees very neatly arranged. She was this elegantly dressed, cotton saree loving, village beauty, who believed that the best jewellery one could wear was a smile. She had long thick hair which was plaited half way from its length downwards. When she smiled, her cheeks had cute dimples. There was also a small dent in her chin. To enhance her beauty, there was a small mole on her cheek.

Another feature of the house that Selina noticed was that there was no prayer room in this house. Bags of rice, lentils, and other grocery items were stored in one room, which also had a loft for unused things. In the courtyard, there was a tulsi plant, and the walls had small dents where lamps were lit in the evening. One entire wall was adorned with black and white pictures of ancestors. Another wall had family photos, which were from various time periods. Near Grandpa's easy chair was a small table with Grandpa's diary and planner.

Everyone had finished bathing and sat down to eat. Here, one must sit on the floor to eat. Food was served on a banana leaf. The meal included *vallarai keerai kootu* (Spinach and lentil gravy), *vazhaithandu poriyal* (steamed Banana stem), *chinna vengaya sambar* (Stallions sambar), and *appalam* (lentil chips), *Arisi appalam* (rice chips), *kappai appalam* (tapioca chips), which were Selvy's favourites. As she was scanning to see if there was a sweet dish, Yegna said, "*Paalada payasam* with *thengai paal* (coconut milk based dessert) and *vellam* (jaggery)." Their neighbour, Baira, had brought it.

Within six months, she had understood that a foreign country was like popcorn you ate at the theatres. You imagine it to give you the experience so romantic as in movies, that countries abroad are clean and that it would smell like the best bouquet. But as soon as you land there, you realise it is like that popcorn that becomes tasteless beyond the fifth fistful. The smell you associated with it was because of the room freshener that the multiplex used while you watched the movie at the theatre. It was clean because many foreign countries were 'fine' countries, or the cinematographer of that movie who shot at the location was extremely talented. It is a Star Hotel, where everything is clean because you pay so much for the services. And anyone who violates is 'fined'.

The unpolished, open-cooked red rice made her realise that even rice had a taste. Every bite, every dish gave her tingling sensation in the mouth. It was as if it woke the taste buds up from the coma stage they had been in from the protest against bread and soups. The taste buds had now urged her to chew more, and slowly. She felt as if her tongue would only let her swallow the morsel after they tasted enough till the whole thing became semi solid.

She ate much more than she had ever eaten all her life and even felt crows would pick the last morsel she had eaten, if she opened her mouth.

*Chiththi* brought her the *payasam* and *vadai*. She said, "push in whatever stands till your neck with the *vadai* and flush it in with the *payasam*." Selvy ate that too.

Selvy felt intoxicated and reached a food coma. She couldn't control herself. The *oonjal* (swing) was the ultimate heavenly place, she thought, and she saw flashes of a person visiting her grandmother.

She saw the cheerful Prof. Bala; she had never seen before. The visitor came with two huge folders. She could hear him saying in her dreams, "we would somehow bring this truth out, *Amma*. The whole world must know the greatness of Tamil, *amma*."

When Selvy woke up, the whole family, *Paati, Thatha, Chiththi, Amma,* sand... Sendhan, and even *Appa,* were sitting on the cane sofa having coffee. It was the aroma of the coffee that had woken her up. She was excited to see her dad and Thatha. They both got along like school besties each time they met.

*Thatha* had an IAS coaching centre at Tirunelveli. He came once a month for a week to Aral. Since Appa was an IRS officer, they had their common topics.

After the coffee and the cuddling with *Appa* and *Thatha,* she went to Anandavalli *chiththi,* who wanted to talk to her. She said she wished to take Selvy out the next day. Selvy also wanted to go to a place where she could escape from the nagging Sand–Sendhan and the gloomy *Paati.*

CHAPTER EIGHT

# The Coin

Selena's family had moved to Gwalior. The perks of having a dad in a transferable job was to get to travel to different cities and experience different cultures. School excursions were a complete waste of time, Selvy thought. They were at the Gwalior Fort. They had to walk a lot and that too in scorching heat. Yegna had packed dry snacks, assuming it would be less messy. But Selvy felt curd rice would have been better in that heat. She had finished drinking 1 litre of water in less than an hour. Sandy and Selvy were 5 years apart. The only advantage of trips like these, was the relief from mothering him all the time. Trips were always class-wise. So, she had to only carry her bag.

The teacher was talking with a lot of enthusiasm about the revolt of 1857, and Rani Laxmi Bhai of Jhansi and the importance of the Gwalior Fort. Selvy grew up mostly in North India, and she always took pride in the valour of the kings in the North. To her, the kings in the north established vast empires, and that is what made them the greatest. She thought about how crowded these grand forts would have been. How would the warriors have been. what their lifestyle would have been. How did the kings interact or instruct his subjects, soldiers etc. Were they like today's politicians, how did that authority sound like? Just by looking at the swords and guns that were there, she imagined what kind of training those warriors would have undergone and how many people would have been needed to maintain the fort. She wondered if they had gathered daily to clean and polish it. The forts were magnificent and, though they had to walk; she wondered how it would have been during those times, when the kingdoms flourished.

She also thought about what the kings and royal family members would have eaten, whether they wore gold and silk every day. While sleeping, did the queens adorn themselves like her mother did, were there night clothes? Did they wear sarees or salwar kameez? She imagined the royal family members depicted in the paintings there, picturing them in such modern day attire, and found herself smiling at the thought.

She was also curious about North Indian Kingdoms, especially Rajasthan with so many forts, having India's desert. Only if a Raja ruled prosperous land, he could have been rich. And wondered if all the funds had been used in the building of forts and for fighting battles. She wanted to ask her teacher, but she also felt, how does that matter? What is the use of knowing history? It's a period that's over and done. She told herself that she should try and contribute to creating history as a scientist.

She saw some young couples hiding behind some of those walls. Her classmates were all giggling at the sight. She then saw one of them write Bhoj and Babitha and draw a heart around it with an arrow. She thought to herself, 'modern day inscriptions... Stone inscription urge was in the genes may be... '

Her friend and classmate Rajat Rathore called Selvy. He was quite close to her. She was suddenly feeling uncomfortable. She sensed something and saw him hiding something behind his back. He was visibly blushing. Selvy actually liked him and had been secretly waiting for this day. Though she always overreacted in a friendly way so that her heart doesn't open up before knowing what he felt.

She asked as if she was his elder sister, "Yes Rajat, tell me.'

He passed on a greeting card. A 3-D one that opened to reveal a single rose. Her eyes were scanning it and she was fighting her welling eyes...

It read... Samyuktha... I love you...

Selvy couldn't control her tears. And since Rajat was her friend, he could sense her disappointment... he suddenly started feeling like an alpha male.. the class topper, the teacher's pet, the one who was the star performer of the school, was in love with him...

But he actually didn't find Selvy attractive at all... Selvy was the dusky skinned girl who never made any efforts to beautify herself. She had always braided her oiled hair, conforming to the school rules. Samyukta was this bollywood inspired stylish girl.

He blurted.. "*tune kaise Maan liya ke thujse koi ladka propose karega. Kabhi aainaa dekha hai*!! How did you assume someone would get attracted to you? Have you looked at yourself in the mirror!!"

His words were more hurting than the card. She managed the situation by saying, "hey silly fellow. I am only excited for you, *Bhai*. This would reach the class beauty. *Samjo pat gayi,* believe that the job's done..." And she winked.

She wanted to use the washroom, but had to wait until they could get back to school. That 1 litre within an hour had filled her bladder straight, without quenching the thirst, she thought.

She rushed to the toilet as soon as they reached school and quickly came back before her friends could look for her and tease her about it.

She didn't want to look at mirrors or speak to anyone after whatever Rajat told her. She wanted to head home and cry...

The class assembled for dispersal after everyone had brought their school bags. They had gone on a half-day trip. CBSE schools were always like that. Some of her classmates came and stood behind her, closer than they usually did. She didn't know why. They were waiting till Yegna came. And they came behind her till Selvy got into the car. Sunitha stepped forward and told her mom something secretly. Selvy was tensed if they were telling mom about Rajat.

Selvy had attained puberty.

Their neighbour had a Saint(*Sadhu*) visiting them, they had Sunderakhand recitation. It was common practice in Gwalior to host people around and read Sunderakhand chapters from Ramayana. They invited Yegna as well. Anandan and his family were not religious. But they weren't atheists. They went to any house they were invited to. Yegna was the enterprising one who would just need a reason to make friends.

Yegna had gotten to know something that gave her a weird feeling. She suddenly felt older. She was always proud about her beauty and youthfulness. Yegna was usually cheerful. But today she suddenly felt the shyness she felt when she met Anandan for the first time. Flashes of her pregnancy confirmation, the first time she held Selvy, the *mottai* and *kaadhu kuthu* (tonsuring of head and ear piercing) of Selvy, were running in her mind like a dream as she was alighting the staircase.

She wanted to get into her house before neighbour Neeti could see them; she thought. As soon as they entered, Yegna asked Sandy to stay in the living room and pulled Selvy into her room. She asked her about how she felt, if there were stomach cramps of any kind and about bleeding.

Selvy was sharp, her friends had already taught her about puberty and she said, "*amma* I noticed nothing." And realised that she had been in such a hurry to use the toilet. The Indian toilet in her school was dark and she had hardly noticed. In fact, she didn't even think remotely of this.

Yegna saw her soiled uniform in the mirror's reflection. She asked Selvy to bathe and hurriedly came out of the room, went to hers and returned with something hidden in her *dupatta*. Sandy was watching TV and thankfully didn't notice. She went into Selvy's room and shut the door. She helped Selvy learn to use the Sanitary napkin and taught her some personal hygiene.

Yegna didn't want to share this with her neighbour till the *sadhu* left. The neighbour aunty came home when the bhajans began and invited them to come, saying it would be over soon. Yegna had by then begun making '*UlundhanKali*' (the urad dal sweet ball) for Selvy. She told Neeti that she would join in 5 minutes.

The *Sadhu* called Yegna after the bhajan and gave her a coin. The *Sadhu* gave everyone 5-rupee coins from his cloth pouch. But what Yegna received was an old-looking copper coin, bigger than the 5-rupee coin everyone got. He told her to give the coin to Selvy when she was 22 years old, "not before that," he insisted. Yegna saw the coin. It was a weird-looking coin with circles inscribed on it. She thought it was a copper coin from sometime in BC.

Neeti was busy seeing off some guests.

Yegna didn't have time to ask her about why she received something else. Neeti then came to her and said, "*Yegna di, jo bhi Sadhu Ahir Maharaj ne diya, haldi lagake is peele kapde mein baandh ke godrej me rakhiyo.*" She kept the coin tied in a yellow piece of cloth and kept it in her locker. Her neighbour mentioned that doing so would bring Lakshmi(wealth) to the house.

Thankfully, it was Friday that Selvy had her first day. Yegna had called all their relatives to share the news and Selvy felt as if she had delivered a baby. Embarrassed beyond words.

Sandy understood nothing. She then said, "Sandy, don't touch *Akka* for three days." Sandy asked, as he overheard the conversation Yegna had with everyone, "you said *Akka* has become a big girl, but she is the same now!"

Yegna didn't even acknowledge that question and changed the topic and began asking Selvy about the trip. Sandy interrupted several times to share that his friend had broken the pencil tip, or that another had eaten his salad, etc.

Anandan came back from office, with all of Selvy's favourite sweets he had bought on his way back. He came to Selvy and touched her head, saying, "*nalla iru da chellam.*" Be well dear.

He then went to the kitchen and stealthily hugged Yegna. Yegna had tears rolling down her cheeks. Anandan whispered in her ear, "*azhagi, Monday pasangala school ku anupchutu padathukku porom enna? Office la leave sollitten.*" (Let's go to a movie when kids go to school on Monday, beauty. I have taken a day off). he gave her, cadbury nutties. her favourite chocolate.

Yegna felt so happy. She wondered how Anandan sensed her insecurity and fell in love with him all over again. Eventhough Yegna was a devoted mother, these subtle emotional expectations about needing her husband's acknowledgement at certain moments, were things Anandan did naturally. She cried tears of Joy, proud of her Love, her man, Anandan.

They sat down together to watch the Filmfare awards on TV. Shah Rukh Khan and Saif Ali Khan were bullying R Madhavan. They ask Madhavan why he had no surname. And everyone, the crowd too started laughing.

Sandy asked his dad, "*Appa,* even my classmates were asking me the same thing, why don't we have a surname?"

Anandan said, "Surnames usually refer to the caste"'

"What's that?" asked Sandy.

Anandan took a minute to think and Yegna pitched in, "Based on the job one does, caste was decided. If you are a soldier or warrior, the names would have Verma, or Singh or Rajput, etc."

"Yes, even Rathore..." said Yegna.

Selvy felt a sting... but didn't show...

"But my classmate Neel Verma's dad owns a sweet shop," said Sandy.

Anandan continued explaining, "Exactly kanna, when they made those surnames, there existed a society based only on profession. The entire society had agreed to send their children to the *Gurukulam* at the age 7 and a ceremony was organised for that. The children learnt unique skills based on individual capacities. They were segregated based on talent within one or two years. When they entered this *Gurukulam*, they lost their parental kulam and were assigned a *Gurukulu* name.

After 12 years, which is 5 years of schooling at the *Gurukulam*, the parents adopted the children. But this time, the adoption was based on job skill. A boy who was extremely studious was adopted by parents who were running *gurukulams* everywhere.

It taught them only things that they can do best. Those who were strong, athletic, and interested in sports or strength training were adopted by soldiers' families. If they were skilled artisans, artists adopted them. Those who had excellent communication skills were adopted by businessmen. If they could tell the difference between food that had salt and were interested in helping to make food, cooks adopted them. When they adopted this way, there was no guarantee that a parent would get their own biological child. This was when society was equal in terms of money and dignity of labour."

"*apdina*?" asked Sandy. "What does dignity of labour mean?"

Yegna said, "respect for any job one did. They felt every job was as important as the other."

Anandan took over, "see *Amma* doesn't go to office. But do you think she is less important at home? She has taken up a responsibility that I can never do as efficiently as she does. A woman can do things that men can never do. Only a woman can bear a child. We cannot bear pain at all. Only women can take care of children. I don't even know how to ask if someone has eaten. I can talk only based on discussion. *Amma* can read from your face if you are sad or happy. So she needn't do things that men do. In fact, she can do things men can never do."

Selvy felt so feminine with that. She had always been thinking her mother's role was less important. She always felt 'unambitious women were unsuccessful', and that was something lowly. And for the first time, she saw how Anandan looked at things. He had been such a perfect man. Selvy used to wonder why *Appa* never forced *amma* to have a career and why *amma* was at home. She understood now that he had let her choose.

Anandan now continued, "So, everyone had surnames based only on their job. Slowly, the society changed when some of them refused to send their children to the *Gurukulam* because they felt too attached to their children. They felt they could teach the skill that they have to their child."

Yegna brought the dinner plates to the hall. Anandan continued taking the plate, "So slowly the names that were job names became caste names. Even worse, people started feeling one job was better than the other. Dignity of labour was lost."

Anandan asked Sandy, "Do you think that the security uncle's job is important?"

Sandy replied, "yes, he takes care of us when we sleep."

Anandan said, "very good! What about that aunty who cleaned toilets?"

Sandy thought for a moment. He had seen that aunty being asked to stay away by the security, wait till *Appa* left and then let her in.

Anandan said, "she is also important. But when society stopped giving their children and became selfish, discrimination began."

"We belong to the State of Tamil Nadu," said Anandan with such pride.

Sandy corrected, "*Appa* we are in Madhya Pradesh."

Anandan continued, "True whole of India is our country. We must consider all places as our own. '*Yaadhum oore yaavarum KeLir*'. But we can never forget our mother land or our own language. There was a leader in Tamil nadu, by name *Aringar* Anna."

Selvy asked, "Appa is he the person whose name has been used as '*Anna*' everywhere in Chennai?"

Anandan nodded and continued, "yes dear. He chose the name for our state as Tamil 'nadu'. No other state in India is called a country. Anna University, Anna flyover, Anna Arivalayam, etc are named after this great man. His name was C.N.Annadurai. He naturally became the Anna for the political leaders."

"When he spoke to the people during his political rallies, he suggested we could stop using surnames. He said let us Tamils set an example of how a progressive society should be."

"Our grandparents felt that was the right thing and after the 1960s we have stopped using surnames dear," said Anandan with a Tamil pride the children had never seen before in him.

Sandy was excited about all that he had learnt. So was Selvy. They felt really proud about their land.

As a studious kid, she was always the teacher's pet, and no one messed with her or had ever asked her about her surname. Selvy never thought that not having surnames could be something one could take pride in. She felt very happy about her little brother who had just started schooling but had so many questions in his mind.

Renuka *Akka*, Anandan's sister, called on Yegna's mobile. Yegna told her about Selvy. She said she didn't want to call them since it would be too early in the morning in the US. She shared with her about the mysterious 'coin' that the Sadhu had given. Renuka asked if she talked about it to her mom, Rajam. Yegna said "yes, of course! I did."

Rajam was a Numismatics researcher. She did not associate herself with any institution. It started as a hobby and then she pursued it seriously. Renuka was curious to see the coin. She was a gynaecologist by profession but had attended courses on epigraphy.

She asked enthusiastically, "does it have some year engraved?"

Yegna said, "I don't know ka. It was not a shiny coin. I think it is copper. I am not sure. It is black."

Yegna took a picture of it and shared it on WhatsApp. There seemed to be some inscription, but it wasn't clear on a photo. Renuka asked her to save it and not polish it. She said she would look at it when she came to India.

Renuka's husband, Dr. Shah was a material scientist who initially worked in the Geology Department, University of Madras. They had recently moved to the US after he joined NASA. He was an expert at his field and could guess the elements in an ore, by mere glance.

Dweepa said, "please let me talk to Selvy..." in a squeak of excitement... Yegna handed the phone to her and knew the phone wouldn't be returned until the battery died.

Selvy told her everything that happened... everything....

When she put the phone down, Selvy was weeping.

The phone buzzed. It was a message from Dweepa... It was a YouTube link of "Who says..." by Selena Gomez.

Selvy heard it on repeat mode for the next three days.

Everytime she sang *la na na na... who says...* Yegna continued... "*sandhippomaa. Oru murai sandhippoma...*" Yegna was a Rahmaniac who felt this song reminded her of a movie song composed by the Oscar winning Music director, A.R.Rahman...

CHAPTER NINE

# Jallikkattu Protest

"All roads are blocked because of some protest at Marina," said the driver. "Selvy *papa*, can I take you back home? Seems like you wouldn't be able to go for tuition."

Selvy was in Grade 11 and was attending IIT-JEE and NEET entrance exam coaching classes after school. She stayed at her paternal grandparents' house in RajaAnnamalaipuram. She had to go to Adyar for her classes. Selvy called her dad, Anandan, in Delhi now, for advice and Anandan suggested they could head back home.

Selvy had completed her 10$^{th}$ in Delhi and joined a school in Chennai for her 11$^{th}$ and 12$^{th}$. Anandan insisted on that. He felt Chennai was always the intellectual capital of India. He wanted her to either join IIT, Madras or Anna University. Even though he was a progressive person, he couldn't risk his daughter being anywhere else other than Tamil Nadu in her prime years.

Anandan decided on this after a lot of oscillation. He recalled how bad he felt when Selvy was with his parents and his sister when Yegna had to complete her master's degree. She had become so fond of her athai that she hadn't even called him Appa. She referred to Renuka's husband as Pappa, just like Dweepa did. But that was when she was a toddler. Now, as a teenager, it would be safer for her to be in Chennai, he thought. Safety of his daughter mattered more than emotions now.

Selvy was already a focussed child. She had set her mind to do software engineering. But she liked biology and wanted to keep that, too. She had visited athai in the US. Dweepa's dad Dr. Shah, had a significant impact on her. Among the men she interacted with, he was the most affectionate, openly displaying love and giving Selvi the same level of importance as Dweepa. He was an important reason for her interest in the fields of physics and chemistry. He belonged to a Gujarati family that lived near Renuka Athai's house. He fell in love with and married Athai with the consent of both families. He was currently a specialist in the field of Material Sceince at NASA. Shah Pappa took her to his research lab, where she realized that her interest was in particle physics. Shah Pappa talked to Selvi about CERN, and from that day on, her only goal became to join the CERN research facility. She thought that studying computer engineering would be the right path for that and worked with complete dedication.

At Delhi, Sandy was watching the Marina protests on TV. He was in grade 6 and had faced enough bullying that he was looking for every reason to establish Tamil Pride. They called him '*Kaalu*' meaning dark skinned. He listened to every programme about Jallikattu and had grown to be a Tamil fanatic. He hated his westernized name.

He had learnt to be a rapper and a beat boxer. He started making songs too, Anandavalli was the source of that acquired gene, thought Yegna.

Sandy wanted to change his name. He pestered his parents to get that changed. Anandavalli had suggested Sendhan. And there was no second thought. He asked his name to be changed officially everywhere.

Selvy was in the capital of Tamil Nadu preparing hard to get out of India as soon as possible. She was an animal activist who thought *jallikattu* was barbaric.

She felt the intellectual capital shouldn't fight for things that cavemen had been practising. She had to miss classes for many days. But she didn't need any extra motivation to study at all. The breaks helped her allot time to learn about particle physics.

She was miles ahead of her classmates all the time but was considered an outcast, since she couldn't enjoy Tamil movies or Tamil songs. She only knew Bollywood and English songs. She spoke like a North Indian. Her spoken Tamil wasn't bad. It had been similar to the one her mom spoke. It didn't get corrupted with the local words like '*chance-e-illa*' or '*sama*' replacing all words that described awe. For Selvy, '*romba nalla irukku*' was the only term that meant really good.

Sendhan was at the country's capital exploring his roots. He went to Aralvaimozhi during the summer vacation and learned, Indian martial arts, *silambam* and *kalari payattu*. Since Aralvaimozhi was closer to the Kerala border, he had access to both. He felt Anandavalli chiththi knew everything under the sun. He grew up with Anandavalli till he was 5.

Anandan's job transfers between Patna and Ahmedabad happened while Sendhan was born. So after Sendhan turned one, Yegna left him with Anandavalli and took him after they settled in Ahmedabad. Sendhan could still recite the Thirukkural. Selvy hated Thirukkural since they tortured her with it. Her grandmother expected her to memorize the whole 1330.

Sendhan had to attend extra classes for Sanskrit. Since the grammar lessons in Sanskrit were too tough, he had to go to a teacher two streets away. The teacher was so good that he had completely made language learning easy. He first conducted a 10 day spoken Sanskrit course and then when kids had acquired quite a lot of vocabulary and communication aspects, he began grammar.

Sendhan had the introduction to '*Ashtadhyayi*' the grammar book of Sanskrit, that day. The teacher boasted about the language and explained the wonderful and detailed manner in which grammar had been organised.

Every word had a root word and then verb endings could indicate time of the event, and gender of the person involved. He proudly elaborated *dwivachanam* as Sanskrit was the only language with verbs and words for pairs of things.

He explained that the learned society of the past considered that speaking briefly was a mark of their intellectual superiority. He explained that '*suryakoti samaprabha*' was such a short verse which meant someone whose brightness was equivalent to one crore suns shining.

The Sanskrit teacher also mentioned about a text which when read from start to finish is the story of Lord Rama and from reverse it was that of Lord Krishna.

Sendhan was beginning to imagine that Sanskrit was superior to Tamil. However, he was torn between his love for Tamil and Tamil Nadu and the Sanskrit language. He thought he would discuss this with chiththi too because she always said, "*Yaamarindha mozhigalile tamizh mozhi pol inidhaavadhengum kanom.*" meaning of the languages she knew, there was no language sweeter than Tamil.

As soon as Sendhan reached home, he asked Yegna about the act of talking as briefly as possible. Yegna patiently listened to all that Sendhan had to share and then calmly responded.

Yegna asked, "Are you talking about poetic reversal alone?" She was thinking of the level of coding her sister had explained about in Tamil literature. She told Sendhan, "In Tamil you have a text that has the same words, the same meaning, but can be interpreted as a book of lifestyle and as an advanced science book. How about that?"

She continued, "In Tamil, we consider even one letter a word. Can you shrink something further?" she asked. It excited Sendhan whenever he had arguments in favour of his belief system.

Yegna began with things Sendhan would know. She asked, "how would you say 'you' in Tamil?" Sendhan replied, "*Nee.*" Sendhan understood what she meant.

She then said, "'*ko'* means *arasan*/king, '*aa*' means/cow *pasu*.." Sendhan continues with enthusiasm, "'*poo*'-flower, '*po*'- go, '*thA*'-give, '*vaa*'-come..." and they continued their game of finding single letter words in Tamil.

CHAPTER TEN

# Naduvu Nilaimai

Geneva, February 2022

At CERN, there were some parts which were open to the Public. It was common for events to take place that would raise awareness among children and enthusiasts about the scientific discoveries happening there. All research institutions undertake numerous initiatives to stress why the government should allocate or prioritize funding for them. Many events are organized here as well, including exhibitions, science events, and some hands-on activities where people can participate.

A benefit of such events was that for researchers who experience stress due to workload, seeing people and children, and explaining their discoveries and their significance can profoundly change their perspectives. On that day, a small event called 'Open Day' had been arranged. No matter how much she tried, Selvy had no way to escape it. Among her team, Selvy had the ability to simplify things better than anyone else. She had been tasked with explaining force fields to the audience. Selvy had the advantage of interacting with professors and serious research scholars of a 175-year-old University at the intellectual capital of India, The University of Madras, Chennai.

She never had a superiority complex as an Anna University, Bachelor of Engineering student. She felt it was an opportunity for an undergraduate student to interact with students and staff of another University where research was going on. Besides, her aim was not to get to Silicon Valley through campus placements. Her heart was with particle physics.

She had attended a conference at the Crystallography and Biophysics Department of the University of Madras. There were presentations where Hannah *Akka* had shown animations of how a molecule behaved in the presence of water. They called it a 'Molecular dynamics simulation'. It was like the small experiment she had done at her art class way back during

Sendhan's play school days.

For the open day, Selvy had drawn paper flowers, coloured them with crayons, cut them out and folded petal by petal inwards. She decided to ask a person in the audience to pick a flower and drop it in a bowl of water. The petals would open as if the flower bloomed. After which she would explain this in the context of Particle Physics.

This was an activity Hannah *Akka* had used earlier, to explain about Molecular dynamics simulation. "When proteins are placed in an environment that did not have water, they would hide their hydrophilic amino acids because those were the ones that would bond with water and would have an entirely different structure. But in the body, a protein in a water environment would open like that flower." This was a beautiful way to explain enzyme function, she had thought.

Selvy used the same flower demonstration to talk about particle physics this time. In her explanation, she interpreted the water to be a force field and the folded flower to be a particle, when the force field wasn't included in the equations. So she explained that the force caused by the interaction of water and the paper made sure that the orientation of the petals and the structure of the atom would be completely different.

She had yet another demonstration in mind- water and pepper experiment- to explain force fields. She was a person who could simplify a complex theory with ease.

She was reluctantly demonstrating her 'simplified versions' to the public at the event. The audience cheered and her cheeks were pink with the embarrassment of sudden realisation of all the attention.

Her friends Meena and Lenka were suddenly not on talking terms with each other. Of the two, Meena was closer. It was a tough situation when you know you liked a friend more and can't disclose it.

The three walked together, with Selvy in the middle. They went for a quick bite. Selvy was so busy with cracking the code that she hadn't had time to ask them what the actual problem was. When they went to the stall, she saw Lenka's boyfriend. He was waving at Meena, and she was behaving like a silly teenager, blushing to glory, oblivious of the crowd around.

Selvy was very upset with Meena. She felt Meena was insensitive and tried to attract a friend's boyfriend, but didn't mention anything. When they got back to the room after the long day, Selvy felt tired but wanted to clarify her (mis)understanding of Meena in her head.

Meena said, "Hey Lenka would never get committed to any relationship."

The guy was from Kolkata, Selvy hadn't even noticed that he was Indian. Meena shared her version of the story- whenever Lenka wanted to go out, the three had gone together. It was obvious for an Indian to get excited about another fellow country person especially while living in another land. Most Biharis can speak Bengali, so they began talking to each other casually. Meena realised one day that he was about to propose marriage and had a surprise planned out. He had always spent from his purse for every outing and was about to take out the ring.

Lenka had turned him down, saying she was only looking for a dating partner. Meena had met him so often that she felt bad for him. Like the stories of the Bollywood movies of the 90s, Meena was asked out one day by him. They grew fond of each other. Now Bhasker Bose was officially Meena's boyfriend.

Selvy's head was spinning after this fairy, sorry, weary tale. She was playing the conversation in her head. She had been listening to Ilangai Jeyaraj *ayya*'s Thirukkural speeches and had heard *Naduvu nilaimai* the previous day. He had explained about what this art about staying neutral was and she compared that explanation with her current situation.

She had a mental scale to decide who was right. Lenka, Meena... Lenka... It's Lenka's boyfriend. She wanted to be in a non-committal relationship. She let Meena come along. Meena... Lenka never asked her to accompany, and Selvy knew that even though Meena told her otherwise, she saw Meena's pupils dilate and she knew Meena lied.

Lenka had a boyfriend, be that choice for whatever was Lenka's dharma/ principles of natural intentions. She knows Lenka and Meena. Lenka was the first girlfriend and Meena didn't need to get on their dates at all. Meena is at fault, Lenka's right friendship wise. It felt as if someone closer to her had to be judged as the wrong person. The scales in her head were tilting towards Lenka.

Meena was waiting for Lenka to lose interest or Bhasker to look at her.

Meena was willing to bond, and gain stability, like an ionically bonded... "Sodium. Chloride". She was the Chlorine who had the electron affinity to accommodate...

Like Physics Wallah, Alakh Pandey sir says, "*Chlorine shaadi karta hai, Fluorine sirf dating. Kyonki Chlorine ke paas jagah hai.*" Chlorine would marry, Fluorine would only attract and commit as much as a date. That is the difference between electron affinity and electronegativity.

But Sodium had to bond, that would make it stable, attain the Neon configuration, yet stay as a metal."

All of it fitted perfectly... She now got the clue for the Adhigaram's correlation. It is the $12^{th}$ Adhigaram of ThirukkuraL. She was now sure about the connections and was involved in it with full conviction. She had to complete adhigaram 38 in 6 months; she told herself.

CHAPTER ELEVEN

# Valluvar - Valli

Selvy and Anandavalli were getting ready to leave. Bala called out, “Valli!”, that’s how she called Anandavalli *chiththi*

“*Amma, poitu vandudaren.*” Amma, We are leaving now, Please bless us, she said and touched Paatti’s feet. Selvy wondered why for a small stroll, Valli chiththi had to take blessings. But since Chiththi had touched Paatti’s feet, Selvy had to do that gesture too.

“*Mani osai- ulagukku kekattum,*” she said and blessed *chiththi.*

Selvy and Valli headed to the Poigai dam. Valli chose a place where they could sit and view the scenic beauty of the place. Valli seemed prepared for this. She had a sling bag, the ‘*Jolna pai*’ in Tamil style. She had a folder inside it.

“Selvy,” she began “have you heard of ‘Deknamen’?” asked Valli.

Selvy almost choked at the question, and spilt the water shwewas drinking. She never imagined that Valli *chiththi* could know that. She only thought Valli was an innocent village school teacher. She knew Valli *chiththi* taught science. But knowledge about an Alchemical code was not just shocking, but Selvy sensed there was more.

She asked what she felt about her name? Selvy had never liked it. She knew *Chiththi* had named her. Selvy didn’t want to say anything rude so she kept quiet.

Valli pulled out a paper where she had drawn something. Selvy felt a bit emotional. She had always been closer to her athai since she grew up with her for a while. She didn’t know *Chiththi* loved her so much.

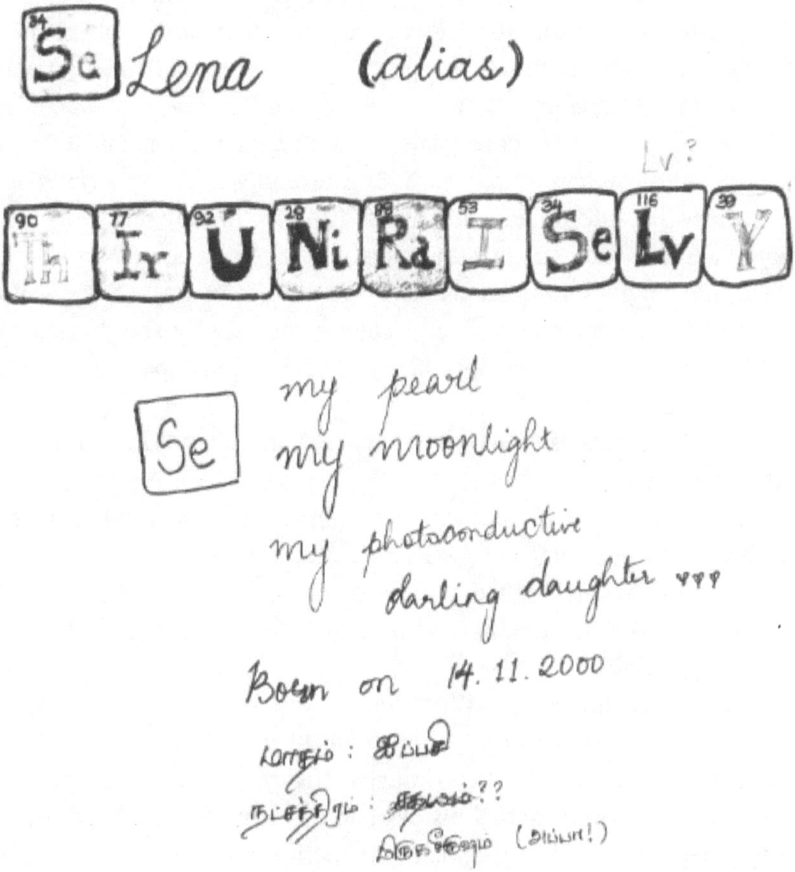


Enter Caption

Valli had made her name with symbols for Elements, Thorium, Iridium, Uranium, Nickel, Radium, Iodine, Selenium, Livermorium, and Yttrium. 'Lv' hadn't been written as an element. She seemed to have added that later. Selvy was highly impressed. She had written about Selenium separately in a corner. My moon, my photo conductive darling. She had also written her date of birth 14.11.2000, and written the Tamil month and star of that day Aippasi- Sadhayam, The star name had been striked out and above that was written Mirugasirusham. She had also written " Amudha Azhagi" next to it. Selvy felt so silly to have changed such a meaningful name. But she felt better about having chosen Selenium of the elements that formed her name.

Selvy sipped a little more water after breaking down into tears after going through the hand made card. She carefully and respectfully placed it back into the file folder and gave it to chiththi and said in a cracked emotional tone, "will you give it to me after we return home?'

Anandavalli got emotional as well. She looked up at the sky, swallowed her tears through her eyelids, and placed the file back into her bag. 'I 'll keep it safe till you are here. Shall give it to you when you are packing your bags.' she said affectionately.

After a few minutes of awkward silence, Valli asked ' Do you remember *Aathichudi* and *Avvaiyar etc?'*

Even though Selvy did her schooling entirely in North India, she had at least heard of *Aathichudi* and *Avvayar*, thanks to her stints in Chennai.

Selvy immediately replied, ' I do remember seeing a black and white movie with an old lady holding a walking stick singing to Lord Muruga. That is Avvaiyar, right?'

Valli laughed and said, "What would you kids do? Many think K.P. Sundaramabal is Avvaiyar. The entire world only learns history through tales and movies. What is more strange is that many don't even understand the difference between actual history and these mythologies and they have as different picture of history painted in their minds."

She then takes out a sheet of paper. Valli was really well prepared for this. There was a clip-on pad on which Selvy placed the paper and Valli gave her a pen.

She said,'Just write whatever I ask you to. I hope you remember the Tamil alphabets'.

Selvy immediately said, "yes *chiththi,* dictate."

Valli said,

"*Aram Seiyya virumbu*

*Aaruvadhu Sinam*
*Iyalvadhu karavel*
*Eevadhu vilakkel*
*Udaiyadhu vilambel*
*Ookamadhu kaividel*
*En ezhuthu igazhel*
*Yerpadhu igazhchi*
*Aiyam ittu uN*
*Oppuravu ozhugu*
*Odhuvadhu ozhiyel*
*Owyiyam pesel*
*Akhan churukkel."*

She said, don't underestimate this poem taught for kindergarten children to be harmless rhyme. It is an alchemical coded text. Selvy had prided herself to be the Sherlock Holmes of her family and an expert at decoding things. Her ego was shattered with every thing that Anandavalli chitti was sharing.

She then explained how to approach this as an alchemist. "If I told you, *Aram sei,* which mean stay true to your virtue, has to do with metallic nature. *Sinam,* which means anger, was extreme heat. Can you try to interpret the *Aathichudi*?" Valli explained the subtlety of understanding this secret poem. "'Aram' refers to a good deed, duty, or prescribed action. You might wonder about the connection between chemical elements and Aram/virtue? Think along these lines. In certain texts like the Thirukkural, the action that is esteemed as highest virtue is referred to as the act of benevolent donation referred in Tamil as 'eegai,'. The term 'aariyya sinnam' translates to camed anger = rage = fire, and the way fire/ anger is calmed is by cooling it off. Try to analyze 'Aathichoodi' as a secret verse by breaking it down and interpreting it," she said.

For Selvi, this was surprising and it was also a moment when her pride was shattered to pieces. Valli's thoughts and intellect completely dismantled her previous impression of her, which she had held in ignorance of her greatness. She surrendered to Valli, accepting these insights. Overwhelmed with emotion, Selvi's eyes welled up with tears.

Valli gently coaxed her, saying, "Oh dear! What happened, Thangam! You were born to take on this task, my darling! Until I lead you to the threshold of this path, it's my responsibility. If you understand its importance, my life will be fulfilled. Based on what I explain, I will open a path for you. May my ancestors of Tamil, my grandmother's wisdom, Ayya Valluvar, avvai and my mother assist me." With that, she raised her hands to the sky, closed her eyes for a minute's prayer and began her explanation.

"*Aram seiya virumbu-* Aram as a supreme Virtue- that is, donating, is regarded as the nature of the metallic elements. Specifically, it refers to the true metals listed among the s-block metals. These metals, in order to be asa stable as the noble gases, are eager to release an electron from their atomic shells. Noble gases are those elements that possess the electronic configuration that helps them operate independently, without interacting with other elements? This stable state is what metals desire to exist in. They are eager to donate their electron or they aspire to perform the highest virtue(Aram),' meaning if you wish to be a true metal, be ready to donate your electron."

*Aaruvadhu sinam.* -"How are metals usually purified? In fact if you consider anger as the rage of fire, and translate this sentence to cooling off of fire, the smelting in fire of an ore and cooling it thereafter may be inferred."

"Iyalvathu Karavel" – Give as much as possible, meaning a metal will only share its valence electrons.

"Eevathu Vilakkel" – One must give without bias. A metal bonds, by sharing electrons with various elements, whether they are other metals or non-metals.

"Udayathu Vilambel" – Do not boast about your wealth. In chemical terms, for an element its wealth is electrons that are available to bond However a true metal(the S Block metals) wouldn't involve or display all the electrons.

"Ookkamadhu Kaividael" – Always remain energetic. How do metals obtain their lustre and shine ? Isn't it because electrons are hopping from one atom to another? If so, do not lose your drive to reveal your nature as a metal.

"Enna Ezhuthu Ikhazhael" – Always pay close attention to numbers and letters. Keep this sentence in mind. If you understand this, I will elaborate further, said Valli.

"Chiththi, just tell me everything. No matter what challenges this research poses, I promise I will tackle it," replied Selvi, her enthusiasm shining through her eyes.

"Pay attention to the next sentence, "Yerpadhu Ikhazchi." Selvi immediately understood. "Chiththi, if that's the case, this sentence is against the nature of metals. That is, for a metal to be formed would be considered a degrading act, right? Then what about the previous sentence? Chiththi, this sounds like a terrible secret language!" she said, looking astonished. In a secret language, when a detail comes that is unrelated to a statement being made, it is expected that the next statement may contradict or completely convey a different message. It's similar... Isn't "Aathichudi" truly a mysterious poem, Chiththi?

Valli really felt relieved and proud. "You have understood this sentence correctly? When a True metal accepts electrons, it will lose its noble gas property as its weight expands outward. Did you see this different dimension of the previous thought!", Valli said.

"Iyyam Ittu Un" – One should share their resources with someone sitting right beside, atleast ask if they are needy somehow. this is the societal virtue. This explains the reactive nature of Metals. They always try to donate electrons to a non metal, as soon as they encounter one in the vicinity.

"Oppuravu Ozhuku" –Bond with elements to create compounds or 'build relationships'. In chemistry, however, this is explained through how some true metals get involved in compounds which expand their valencies without actually chaning their nature. examples of this are Boron hexafluoride. You might recall that Boron has a valency of 3. However, two molecules of Boron trifluoride exist as the hexafluoride so that the electron affinities are balanced.

"Othuvathu Ozhiyel" – Again, I leave this sentence for your research."

*Awviyam pesel*- Don't gossip. Conversation refers to formation of bonds. So, gossip is illegitimate talk, which would involve secrecy. Thus, gossip here could refer to using d or f orbitals to expand the valency to dangerously unnecessary levels. to form colloidal compounds. You might recall that in these coordinate covalent bonds are formed and these compounds are like colloids. neither clear solutions nor solids. they are fluid. which is exactly how gossip would be also. It is like a slippery talk, which could let someone's reputation slip past.

*Akkhan churukkel.* The symbol for alphabet 'akh' has three dots. This could refer to the three sub-atomic particles or... Basically, shrink to that level to realise the truth...You know that metals always like to shrink their atomic radii and mimic the preceeding Noble element, right?"

ஆத்திசூடி - ஔவையார்

Key:-
அறம் = ஈகை
⇒ Giving away electrons($e^-$)

அறம் செய விரும்பு
Be willing to give away electrons like the S- Blk elements, metals. They give away to be as stable as Nobel gases.

ஆறுவது சினம் [சினம் = Anger = Fire]
Cooled after the fiery (anger) ⇒ how metals get extracted.

இயல்வது கரவேல்
Give as many as possible. Valence electrons alone ...

ஈவது விலக்கேல்
Bond with any element. Don't be specific

உடையது விளம்பேல்
Don't show off other electrons or involve them.

ஊக்கமது கைவிடேல்
Excitation (sign of motivation) causes metallic sheen/lustre

எண் எழுத்து இகழேல் ·ᵒ/ₒ
odd statement in the scheme [Possible Gear shift]

ஏற்பது இகழ்ச்சி
If you're a S Blk metal, then accepting electrons is lowly.

ஐயமிட்டு உண்.
Choose ionic/covalent bonding. share electrons if reqd.

ஒப்புரவு ஒழுகு
The above practices would help you stay as compounds

ஓதுவது ஒழியேல் ·ᵒ/ₒ [Next Gear shift]
odd statement in thought flow

ஔவியம் பேசேல்
Don't indulge in Gossip [Don't form coordinate cmpds like D-Blk metals and then it becomes insoluble / colloidal

ஃ·கம் சுருக்கேல் ⇒ ·ᵒ/ₒ reference to Godliness [Annihilat

Enter Caption

Selvy was flabbergasted. She couldn't fathom how Avvaiyaar could hide an alchemical code in a children's rhyme. She didnt know if she should wonder about avvai's intellect or Valli chitti's. How could Valli Chitti have deciphered something as mind blowing as this one! Selvy visualised Valli as the Goddess of knowledge, Goddess Saraswathi, but in copper coloured saree, since she was in the land of Tambraparani, (which meant the cradle of copper), holding the veena with two hands and the third and fourth arms held a volumetric flask and a pipette.

Selvy stared at the sheet that *chiththi* had completed, for over 10 minutes trying to assimilate all that was discussed, and asked, "*chiththi*, are you telling me that Tamil texts could be Decknamens?"

Valli said, "Not just that... Much more," she said. She wanted Selvy to decipher the Thirukkural.

'Shall we go back in time? 'Valli asked. She started with a question again, "Do you know why we stay in Aralvaimozhi of all places we can be in?"

Selvy knew this was about to shake her beyond her wildest imaginations. She was already expecting something fantastic and unbelievable.

Valli began, "This mountain range is called Podhigai. Tamil word Podhi means...", "burden," completed Selvy.

Valli continued, "The podhigai hills are mentioned as '*potiyal, potalaka* etc in ancient texts which are found in China, Japan and in some works of Ptolemy. They mention this mountain as '*Gandhaka malai*' also for the fragrant herbs like cardamom that give it the distinct smell. Do you know what pudhayal is? It means treasure. The word Podigai must have either come from *pudayal, pathukkal, paathukaathal, pothivaithal, poditha malai* etc. which all mean secret and hidden or treasured.

Fun fact, in Malayalam, as part of *Chera naadu*, this place was the mountain of secrets. The chera people said, '*Padukka, Padukka*, meaning careful, cautious, as if there were secrets in here. *Padhukku* in Tamil means to hide or hoard. Have you heard of *Agathiyar*?"

Selvy nodded "yes, only as a name of one of my classmates, Agastya."

"*Agathiyar* is the Father of Tamil. He had the vision of the Tamil language, which was taught to him by Lord Shiva. He has walked on these places we are sitting on right now. Can you believe that? The very thought of this gives me gooseflesh." she said with immense pride. "This is the mountain range from where Tambraparani flows, too. Originally, Sri lanka was attached to our peninsula, and Tamil texts describe the river to have originated in the Podhigai malai and have flown till Sri lanka.

The dam that we are in is to route the Poigai river towards the adjoining villages for irrigation. Poigai is a forest stream. This region is not open for people now. The place has Bears. Note this," said Valli, laying emphasis on the point she was about to reveal. "It is a reserve forest behind these areas. She points to the fence. "The place has numerous caves and thick vegetation. Some labs must be situated in places like these, you see..."

Selvy wondered if the indication was towards CERN.

She then asked, "what do you think are these animals, bears, apes, chimps? Those that stood on two limbs. Right or left-handed?"

Selvy didn't know. She asked,' That's crazy chiththi. Do they even know to tell left from right? Does it have significance in these species? I never even thought of this!'

Valli smiled and began again, "These animals are naturally left-handed. The alchemists of this region were the tribe that had begun using the right hand as well as the right brain. Meaning, they were ambidextrous. Right-handed people have left brain activated; left-handed people have right brain activated."

She asked again, "what do you call the right side in Tamil?" Selvy knew that, she immediately answered, "*Valadhu kai* is right hand so '*valadhu*' is right, right*!!*"

Valli acknowledged and continued, "Perfect! so those who were able to use both hands and had both brain lobes functional were more efficient... they had '*Valimai*-power, *Vallamai*-capability, they were '*Vall'avar*- skilled, ... They are the *Valluvars*, and their women were *Vallis*..."

Selvy looked at her chiththi in disbelief. She seemed to look divine but this time she was in the attire of a tribal woman with a bow and an arrow-quiver on one shoulder and a boomerang like tool on another.

Valli said, "They are the ones... the tribe that knew the past, present and future. They chose the location they wished to stay in. Imagine the map of India. If you stood facing the east, which direction does your right-hand point to? Yes. That's their land. In all three of the major continents. Here it is about the preferences of the century when Valluvar lived. The longitudes were the ones that helped them know the time zones and movement within the longitudinal zones was not restricted. At that time, the seasons and the practices were relevant to the zone they belonged to."

"Did you visit Prague?" asked Valli. Selvy now understood why she had suggested the Alchemy Museum visit, which she had gone to, a week before coming to India.

Valli said "What you saw there was probably the smallest one. This mountain probably hosts many such mysteries. The Siddhars can be encountered in many regions in the South. The Mountain ranges below Vindhyas are their choice, since that was suitable for them and they were not practising skills that buddhist monks were trying to perfect. They were healers. They believed herbs could heal ailments. They said, '*Unave marundhu, Marunde unavu*' 'Food is medicine, medicine is food'.

Sidhdars were trying to achieve transcendental state and were trying to explore the astral space for answers to the mysteries of this world. They were beyond religions. They practised a way of life called '*Aseevagam*'. This was about being one with nature."

Selvy's attention drifted to the new religion she had heard Valli mentioned, she asked about the difference between Aseevagam and Hinduism.

Valli said, "I wouldn't want to dwell on that discussion today. I would quickly tell you with an example of how Aseevagam's simple principle got absorbed into Hinduism and had suddenly become associated with grandeur and show, and now that has become environmentally harmful.'

'Aseevagam had a few symbolic caricatures incorporated. They considered their ancestors as their guides and prayed to them when they were confused about something. Therefore, their gods had human figures with pets or other animals they had mastered, and these were placed on open ground.'

'One symbolic figure that was suggested as a target for people to achieve philosophic superiority, a caricature of sorts is '*Vinayagar*' or '*Pillaiyar*'. What symbolism do you associate with Pillaiyaar? asked Valli.

Selvy said, ' He has the head of an elephant, right?'

Valli explained, 'He is symbolized as one with big ears, long nose and big tummy. Aseevagam's philosophy was similar to the Saiva sidhdhantham. They believed that the creation of the world and the exit of souls from the world were in a specific sequence in tune with the elements of nature. They believed that the Aakasha element was the first to begin and I don't have to tell you what its significance is, I guess. It is akin to the force field.

Whatever we send and receive is through this medium. So, when we utter a word, it is like a manthra. It has three components; it has a force that arises from our muscles that move while uttering it. The force for that comes from our core muscles and our vocal chords. The word also has a meaning and an intention. The sound vibration is the only one we sometimes give thought to and hear. When we speak to a child or a person of a different language, we might sometimes hear their intentions, too. Hear in the sense, not hear per se, recognise.

The eardrum receives sound, but the other two inaudible frequencies linger, since they have set the atoms around the space between the speaker and the receiver in motion. Like waves in water, these would come back. This is what these saints believed in. The intention aspect of the word comes from the gut. It is considered the second brain. Have you heard of gut instinct?" asked Valli, and continued without waiting for a response. "They therefore symbolised a Vinayagar with big ears, capable of receiving signals from Space. A pot belly symbolising one with a larger gut instinct."

Selvy asked, "Why the elephant's face and nose?"

Valli sported a smile of pride, one that a teacher would get when she left an information gap on purpose for the student to capture, and the student pops up with that question spot-on. She explained, "among the 5 elements of nature, air, water, fire, earth, and space, and the five senses and sense organs, there is an eternal connection. So, skin and touch are associated with the air element, vision and eyes are associated with fire, taste and speech are associated with water, Nose and smell are associated with earth."

Selvy clarified with a sense of amazement, "So the nose is for the relevance of these elemental associations with this planet, Earth. Is it *Chiththi*?"

Valli excitedly affirmed, "Exactly! my dear!" Selvy deciphered the rest, "The elephant head then must represent enhanced brain activity. So, these symbols were caricatures with such deep meaning!!" Selvy was taking some time to process all that she heard.

Valli knew it was too much for the kid, but was certain Selvy had that receiving capacity, like the vinayagar...

"So how did the Aseevagam saints pray?" Selvy moved on to her next question.

"Baley! Epdi da chellam, you ask exactly what I am going to mention next..." exclaimed Valli with joy.

"That practice we still continue. What do you do in front of *Vinayagar*, first fold your hands and strike the ends of the forehead with the fist, you hold the right earlobe with the left hand, the left earlobe with the right, and do '*Thoppukaranam*' Or in modern day terminology, 'super brain yoga'? This is an exercise for activating the two lobes. It is also a core exercise as a squat. So, it activates the two thought centres, the brain, and the core."

Valli continued, "there are colloquial expressions when people say,' *pidichu vecha pillayar*', meaning it can be symbolically made with a mound of anything, clay, turmeric, dough, even dung. And to worship for these powers, they offered flowers and leaves. They had the practice of lighting lamps, but never believed in '*Homam*' where a fire pit was created. They loved nature, and they believed in offering things with water to accompany them so that they could dispose off things in rivers and lakes, for the fish and other animals to consume too."

The day chosen for *Vinayaka chathurthi* is in the month dedicated to ancestor worship, called *Purattasi*. It is on the fourth day of the waxing moon. Since usually moon is noticeable only on the fourth day. When there is darkness, the moon is considered the guiding light. Before the rainy season, they desilt the ponds and rivers to create an idol of Lord Ganesha using the soil, mixing in 21 types of medicinal leaves. This clay idol is then placed in water. When the rains come, the clay coats the water bodies and helps to retain the rainwater. The medicinal leaves serve as a remedy for certain physical ailments that spread through water. When we enter winter and days become shorter, we exercise on that day to stay alert and not feel sleepy. I don't have to tell you what *Vinayaka chathurthi* of today is..."

Selvy sat with her head down with her hands around her folded knees... After 15 minutes, Selvy asked, "Is this why *vasam*, which means smell is used for a place of living, did that become '*maNam*', another word for smell, and staying together, '*Thirumanam*'?"

Valli turned and took Selvy's hand, kissed it, and uttered with confidence, "*Nee mudichuduva da thangam*... You would finish the work, dear, I completely trust it now."

Valli said, "it is getting hot dear, let's make a move."

Selvy asked about what *paati* had said when they started, about *MaNi*, "Is that some bell?" she asked. Valli's chest swelled with pride, "She said, that's where we are heading to."

There was a Christian shrine in Aralvaimozhi. It was in fact the cemetery of a minister from a Chera Kingdom, who had got influenced by the Dutch sailors and had converted to Christianity. When the king came to know of it, he banished the minister and he died at this place," told Valli.

That sounded pretty weird as a story. And now that she knew who her chiththi was, she knew Valli didn't believe a word of that.

Selvy asked, "So what's the truth?"

Valli said, "*pathukka pathukka*... I ll tell you... who else..." and smiled. "Let that wait... Today is for observation. Make note of all things you feel suspicious about. And I would tell you soon.

They went to the bell rock and then returned home."

Valli felt Selvy was overloaded with information so she wouldn't disturb her for a day.

CHAPTER TWELVE

# The Alchemy Museum

Prague, September 2021

Meena was completely busy, smitten... so Lenka had now become Selvy's shopping, eating, and chatting companion. Selvy actually thought Lenka was German but her family had moved to Germany two generations back from Czech Republic. Lenka had a lot of relatives in Czech Republic and when all the topics about each other's school and college life were over, they began talking about their countries, their cultures, etc.

Selvy had begun enjoying Lenka's company a lot. In fact, though Meena and Lenka had their reasons for whatever happened between them, deep inside, Selvy felt that Meena was wrong. In her mind, popped Rajat and Samyuktha, she wondered if they were still a couple.

Selvy had lived all over India, so she had endless stories. But Lenka had exhausted all her experiences. She now needed something to talk about and she began to gossip. She mentioned about her cousin who had been a model and had even taken part in the beauty pageants and had missed being chosen as Ms.Czech republic.

She said that her cousin had dated 5 boys at the same time. She spoke about her house, the cousin's house and how it used to be flooded with products that she had tried just once and a lot of cosmetics trial packs. Lenka said sarcastically, "what needed to be there was a cupboard for condoms. And since that wasn't there, she had conceived thrice and aborted them within 3 years!"

Now Selvy was beginning to feel the gossip was exaggerated beyond necessary. She asked the cousin's name. Lenka said her name was Johanka.

They went out shopping that weekend. Dweepa called Selvy and reminded her about Aakash's birthday. Selvy said that she was going out to shop for his birthday. They both spoke for some time and Lenka had gone to get a cup of coffee for both.

Selvy had shared about Dweepa and about their secret code book that was released the previous year. Lenka asked if Selvy was her only cousin. Selvy smiled and nodded a yes.

Lenka started off again. Her dad's dad had 5 sons, her dad had 4 brothers. Each had a boy and 2 girls. She began telling names of her cousins and there was no Johanka, noticed Selvy.

She then asked Lenka, "who is the beauty queen among the names you mentioned?" Lenka said "Branka". Selvy confirmed that Lenka was lying, but she ignored it.

Their shopping took more time than they expected, and they grabbed some sandwiches for lunch and headed back to their rooms. Selvy realised her wallet was with Lenka.

She then realised when she opened it, that the whole time, the coffees, the sandwiches, the tickets were all bought with Selvy's money. "Lenka is a mystery," thought Selvy.

She had been thinking of asking her to go along to Prague. But now she wondered if she ever had relatives in Czech.

Selvy had to ask Meena only again. Bhasker was a sincere guy. And after Selvy's experience with Lenka, she thought Meena had never been that way. She had always been magnanimous. While thinking about it, Selvy told herself. If Lenka used my money to buy for both of us, and if I feel bad about it, I am being silly, too. Let me be magnanimous, Thirukkural says that too. She had been so inspired by Thirukkural and Valluvar, and she had to thank Ilangai Jeyaraj *ayya* for that.

Bhasker and Meena agreed to come along with Selvy to Prague. Bhasker was really a nice guy. He had booked the tickets. They planned to spend the weekend there. He had even booked two rooms. Selvy thought she would ask him how much she owed after they got back from the trip.

On the way, Selvy observed that Bhasker was transfering money to someone through the phone. And asked Bhasker about it. He said Lenka wanted some money. He was feeling guilty about ditching her for another girl, and so he had been transferring her money whenever she asked. He added, "It's not much Selvy, don't worry."

Selvy got his account details from Meena and transferred her share for the tickets and room expenses immediately.

Selvy was feeling weird. She was extremely confused. There were too many things running in her head. She had needed to prepare for an upcoming conference presentation. Thirukkural and Valluvar were constant companions. It was Selvy's second visit to Prague after getting back from India. She wanted to clear some doubts she had.

"The airport runway is being relaid", said Bhasker. "Oh, is it! What happened?", asked Meena.

Bhasker said "the concrete had cracks. The cracks began spreading. So, they must optimise the cement mix and lay it again. Silicon in Cement is unpredictable. It would neither let go nor bond properly." he said. "Like your ex" added Meena.

Selvy got it. She was stuck at *Adhigaram* 14. Now their connection was clear as quartz, she thought to herself. Silicon sure is unpredictable. It can be a Crystal 'Quartz' too.

At the Alchemy Museum, Selvy was transported into her world of visualisation, she looked at every small bottle and every little detail there. The ceilings had planets symbolized. The lab was through a secret door, underground. There were coins on the floor. There seemed to be more secret knobs to doors or bigger rooms, too. The whole thing must have existed in an area of 2000 Sq ft below. As a scientist at an underground facility, she felt there surely was more than just its being 'secret' as the reason for its location under the ground. What about safety? What about inertness or non-reactive or vacuum requirements?

CHAPTER THIRTEEN

# Padhukka... Padhukka...

Aralvaimozhi

Valli wanted Selvy to process all the information she had heard and not disturb her. But Valli sensed Selvy hadn't completely believed whatever she had said. Valli offered to take Sendhan and Selvy to her school the next day.

Selvy had become overly curious that she started looking for content related to such topics on YouTube. She came across channels that led her to believe all that Valli *chiththi* had told her. She also found content where Tamil scientists abroad shared their thoughts and became doubtful again.

She started wondering if there was scientific evidence to the claims that chiththi made. Proof that can be published in a peer reviewed scientific journal with a good impact factor.

Valli was looking thoroughly excited. Bala *Paati* also began smiling. She didn't want to ask her disturbing questions this time, since that was the first time she had spoken to her at this length. She felt she would, for the sake of her *chiththi*, pretend to be interested in the decoding of Thirukkural. She had nothing major to expect from it.

Valli had been watching Selvy. She then invited her to her school to spend some time and motivate the children. Selvy happily agreed. Sendhan tagged along too. The children were exceptionally bright, Selvy thought. They were independent and mindful.

Valli *chiththi*'s class was like a mini lab. Selvy went to class 7. The children stood up and shouted in a chorus," *kalai vanakkam amma.*" Selvy had been used to, "Good morning, ma'am" and was pleasantly surprised.

Valli began with the attendance, and they were responding with "*uLLen amma.*" And not 'present ma'am'. One name from the attendance list stuck with Selvy, KaNikumaran. She wondered if that was Kanyakumari's male version of the name or was it related to the 'Vishu KaNi', that is celebrated on close to the Tamil New year's day in Kerala.

Valli was teaching the children the process of combustion. She encouraged the children to handle everything on their own.

She asked them to light a match, use it to light a piece of camphor on a plate. She had a small, sealed glass box, and she had a rat caught with a crude trap. She let the rat into the glass box, which had some food, and sealed it. Many girls in the class squeaked before the rat did.

Valli chiththi said, "Don't worry children, nothing will happen. We will finish the experiment quickly and release the rat outside."

She then asked them to observe. Then children were asked to touch the flame and the plate. And, the glass jar. The glass jar was slowly getting fogged up. She then took the glass jar to let the rat out. A boy from the class volunteered to help her, the KaNikumaran. They let the rat out and came back.

She then began explaining how the camphor burnt by asking what the children had observed. A few hands shot up to answer.

One kid who was given a chance answered, "because of the match that lit it." She had blindly said, but that was the right answer.

*Chiththi* then drew the equation of combustion of a fuel. She drew methane and said this would combust and become carbon dioxide and water. The camphor does not have methane, but it contains a carbon compound.

She asked what happened when you touched the plate, and the class sang in chorus. "*Suttuchu* ...miss", it was hot.

She continued explaining that combustion was an exothermic process. Heat is evolved. This is the basis for its use as a fuel.

She then asked what happened in the glass jar, and about feeling the heat there, they all said... "No miss, *adhu sudala miss*" that wasnt hot ...in the same tune as good morning, miss.

She asked why they thought so. One child said, "we didn't light anything there with matches, miss." Another said, "because it was the glass they touched" a lot of random answers emerged. Valli invited Selvy to explain.

Selvy began, living things also do the same reaction. The food in the glass jar was the camphor. The oxygen in the jar before sealing was the matchstick.

The boy who helped the rat, KaNikumaran asked, "*appo thattu edhu ka*?" what was the plate?

"That was inside the rat." answered Selvy. "The reaction inside the rat involved things called enzymes."

Selvy took another camphor, struck a match, and placed it away from the camphor, and then after that struck another and lit it.

She explained, "The plate has the camphor. If you placed the match near it, then the camphor would burn immediately right. So, the enzyme is like that *thattu*, which brings the camphor, the food and the matches, the oxygen in the air near each other and then the reaction happens. These can let this combustion happen without the heat. *Kaathula irukkara oxygen than soodatha eriya vechudhu,* matches start *than panichu.*"

The boy who let the rat out asked, "*akka*, why did the glass jar fog up?"

Selvy was impressed at the observation. She clarified that the camphor was burning in the open, and asked what did it convert to, "What is that, do you remember?" asked Selvy, pointing to the equation on the black board.

A girl answered, "Carbon dioxide."

"Very good", said Valli.

"So, the rat also produced that carbon dioxide after combustion. Since the jar was sealed, you saw the fogging. Whereas in the plate that was open, the carbon dioxide escaped into air", said Selvy.

Selvy tried her best to simplify it. And was amazed at Valli's planning. She sealed the jar on purpose.

Valli told the children to record their observations in their notebook. As Selvy and Sendhan left, Selvy noticed that the children read from the textbook placed upside down. And were writing with their left hand. She knew Valli was training them to be ambidextrous, too.

Valli then took Selvy and Sendhan to Class 12.

On the way, she said, "What you explained is what alchemists achieved. They used the enzymes in herbs, body fluids, and micro-organisms and achieved a combustion, a metal transmutation, a purification that needed a furnace and achieved that without a furnace. They used selenium as a photoconductor. It conducted electricity when there was light. They used silicon as the semiconductor, which responded to slight changes in heat... Intentions and trust are important whenever we begin something dear. Now address the class of 12 and tell them about careers."

Selvy was again blown away by how committed Valli was.

The next day, Sendhan had gone out with the neighbour's son on a trek on the mountain.

Valli and Selvy went to the Bell rock the next day.

Selvy had made a mental list of her doubts. First was the place where Devasahayam Pillai is believed to have kneeled down to pray (it had two big circles and one small circle, like the alphabet- ஃ), the crucifix (it wasn't the usual crucifix that was in the other places). The tear rock, the bell rock, the cave and the trenches, the view, the supposed place where he was shot were all things she needed to talk about. Selvy wanted to know Valli's version of what could have happened before discussing her doubts.

Valli began, "there was a king of the Travancore kingdom, Marthanda Varman. He had fought the Dutch and had won. There were some soldiers who were prisoners of war. Marthanda Varma was specifically impressed with one of them, Eustachius de Lannoy. He had then recruited him in his own army and soon; he won the Maharaja's trust and had become a Commander in the Army. He was also talented in Fortification and had carried out the restoration of several Forts nearby. Since he belonged to a different faith and since he needed easier access to the construction sites, he stayed at Udayagiri, in a Fort. His tomb is in Udayagiri Fort where the stone reads that he was loyal and revered.

This person who died here was a minister Neelakantam Pillai, at the same Travancore kingdom. He grew close to de Lannoy and got influenced by him and converted to Christianity. King Marthanda Varma couldn't tolerate this, and he is believed to have tortured Neelakantan pillai, who was now rechristined as Lazarus, locally, Devasahayam Pillai, and had left him in the region under the Pandya kings, Aralvaimozhi. This man was already bleeding and was left in a wild forest. He seems to have meditated and healed himself.

British soldiers found him and fired bullets and he was 'martyred'. Christian British soldiers 'killed' him.

But there are paintings in great detail about the torture and then banishment by the Maharaja. Now Devasahayam pillai has been beatified by the Vatican. He is 'Saint' Devasahaym pillai. Now shoot your bullets", urged Valli.

Selvy was shocked. She understood at once why Valli wouldn't believe this.

Selvy asked, "when the person who influenced conversion was revered, how can the close aid of the kingdom, a minister, be banished after torture? Seems illogical", she said.

Selvy asked about the cross at the place of shooting. It was different. Valli said. "That's our clue."

Selvy then asked about the knee impressions. "Can such deep impressions be achieved on a rock by a human's kneeling!!"

Valli said, "yes you can! What are you saying? We have stories of somebody's tooth in a temple, somebody's large feet on a rock in another temple, etc."

"*Bade bade deshon mei aisi choti choti baaten hoti hai senorita*" In big countries such small things are common... winked Valli.

Selvy was laughing... She didn't know Valli could speak such good hindi.

"Do you watch Shah rukh movies?" asked Selvy. Selvy didn't, after the surname bullying, she had seen on TV long back.

"As if we 80s-90s kids had a choice", said Valli. "He was my Hindi teacher. I learnt Hindi by watching movies, dear. Otherwise, I would be speaking like your dad, '*Yek gaaw me yek kisaan raghuthatha*" a sentence usually pronounced in a south Indian slang to make fun of the incapacity of the South Indians to pronounce a non phonetic language.

"It's about what you choose to learn from whatever you watch. You can learn Bollywood dance or fashion or... seek the truth. The difference between sight and vision"...

Selvy looked at the knee depression again, "Neelakantan kneeled here" She said. Valli and Selvy laughed till their stomachs hurted.

She then asked about the cross at the place the bullets were fired. It wasn't the usual cross.

Valli said, "no comments... These are things that have gone beyond us."

"The bell rocks?" asked Selvy.

"That's our crucial proof," said Valli.

She then said, "let's go to that point that's 'strategic', " pointing to a place from where the entire valley could be viewed, along with the mountains around.

It was breath-taking, with the natural beauty that marked tradition and heritage, and the windmills. It was like Selvy and Valli.

Valli signalled they could comfortably be seated on the rock walls and said, "we are at the Natarajar silai of CERN, of the glorious time before the Sangam period."

Selvy visualised that, experiencing goosebumps.

Selvi, was filled with ecstasy. She closed her eyes, for a moment and imagined the statue of Nataraja from Chidambaram. She envisioned such a statue here. Valli was dressed like the women of ancient times, and nearby were many revered figures like Valluvar and Avvaiyar. She opened her eyes and looked around; while others vanished, Valli, with her beautiful hair braided hair and dressed in an elegant handloom cotton saree, was sitting majestically.

Valli continued, "These hills have the labs under them. Those that existed for centuries. For the reasons best known to you, as a particle physicist, and the world now, these had to be underground, so that they could carry out advanced research without the disturbance without side effects or radiations leaking out."

"Is that the tear? Nuclear medicine!!" asked Selvy

Valli didn't answer. She paused and continued, "these places of worship are untouchable. And I have no complaints. They have helped preserve all these treasures. The bell rock was the alarm to indicate the scientist inside the lab like the secret knobs you would have seen in Prague."

Selvy had visited it in such a hurry that she didn't notice finer details.

"The bell rock that you see here is supposed to have fallen from the top. All these remnants you see are those that happened in 1756. I am talking about a time at least 7000 years before this," said Valli, with a clenched fist.

She said, "*Ennum ezhuthum Kann ena thagum, Thamirabarani agastya malai*, the Hadron Collider"...

Valli hid the slip of paper she had in her fist. She felt she would give it to Selvy after she was convinced about Valli

"Please visit Rajam *paati* in Chennai, dear. I know you might get convinced after that", said Valli.

CHAPTER FOURTEEN

# Aakash turns 1 on Sivarathiri

Dweepa, unlike Selvy, was extremely social. Selvy was wondering about a cryptologist having so many friends. There were neighbours, colleagues, and a few relatives of her husband, too. And there were people from every nationality.

Renuka *athai*, and Shah Pappa had come. She had to take the day off at the lab. *Athai* shared that Shah uncle had retired and that they would relocate to Chennai. They were leaving for Chennai the next day. And they came to attend the Birthday celebrations en route.

Selvy was feeling insecure. She chose to take care of serving the guests' food. She went and stood near the Barbeque.

Aakash was now standing and so he hated to be carried all the time. It was harder to manage a kid at that stage. So, he was entirely with *athai*.

Selvy was forced to overhear too much, she thought. She never knew that gossip was cross-cultural. She had heard that a bollywood actor was killed, and he had become an agent. That he has written everything as encrypted information and the drives were stolen and are being read by someone on YouTube.

Selvy moved to the next group of gossipers who were discussing the clothes, that Tamil actor Sivakarthikeyan wore a Balmain t-shirt which cost 40,000 Indian rupees, and that another Tamil actor Vijay's branded car wasn't allowed to be brought to India. And about the new OTT released movie, the new Surya movie, that has featured in the Oscar's YouTube channel, etc.

Another circle was talking about Hollywood, Oscars, the slapping and if that was true or Staged etc.

Selvy quickly escaped to Dweepa's husband, Gautham's circle.

She had been thinking that the Merchant Navy was like a cruise ship. And she thought Gautham would be that headstrong, handsome, smart man.

He was 6.5 feet tall, the typical definition of a tall, dark, handsome man. He was muscular, but not the body builder type.

Selvy was surprised that he was extremely kind and friendly. He asked affectionately 'When I am here also you should consider it your right to come home. Not just be here when I am away at work, alright dear?!'. He said, 'Dweepa is always yours.'

Selvy was blushing. He felt so elder brotherly that Selvy felt very comfortable. It was indeed easy to talk to Gautam. He made her feel like he was an elder brother Selvi didn't have. She regretted having misunderstood him. Although there were many friends around him, he was engaging in conversation with each one without letting anyone go effortlessly. Selvy was thoroughly impressed.

Selvy didn't speak much because she was feeling odd about being so judgemental about people. One of Dweepa's friends came and sat next to Selvy and began talking. Selvy thought that would be a good chance to escape from the other gang. She introduced herself as Branka. It reminded Selvy of the beauty pageant winner, Lenka's cousin. Selvy smiled and was thinking she would be from Czech Republic and would probably be Dweepa's neighbour.

Branka was Dweepa's colleague and was taking care of the network department. She told herself to never judge a person with her name.

The Bollywood crazy people, led by Yuktha, started dancing to the suddenly changed party music. There was some *aalaap* , a classical music piece in between some remixed songs and suddenly the table cloth caught fire.

There was a sudden commotion and then people settled and began dancing again for something else.

Savithri aunty, Dweepa's neighbour, commented, "*Deepak Raagam madiri edho pola irukku.*" It must have been a piece from *Deepak Raag*, a classical raga known to be associated with fire. Savitri Aunty said, "Tansen, who was a musician in the court of Emperor Akbar, could ignite fire by singing the Deepak Raaga, and could bring rain by singing the Megh Malhar. There is such a connection between music and nature." She shared thatshe had been a retired professor of Classical carnatic music at a college. After taking a moment to boast about her grandchildren, she mentioned that she was observing a fast that day and that she fasted every Shivaratri. Then she called her grandchildren and quickly took her leave. Since it was Sivarathiri.

Selvy felt the rhyme scheme... Savithri is fasting on Sivarathiri...

Selvy's thoughts drifted to the connection between the *raga* and catching fire. She wondered how this was possible.

The music of planets from Ragam (*Navagraha keerthanam*) was something she had heard. She saw the line spectrum connections as well. She took her phone out and began searching. There was information about atomic resonance frequencies. There was also information about planets and their frequencies. She was thinking the element in the cotton on the tablecloth could have got excited with the resonance frequency of the raaga.

She checked again about the raga. Looked at the notes and those that coincided with the atomic resonance frequency of it. And she found a match, 'a Match'. Anything about catching fire had a 'Match' too.

She then checked if this note had been something important. She found that Classical Carnatic music had classified notes of a raga as Jeeva swara. Or swaras that bring out the life of the raaga. She was stunned to see that the Jeeva swara of raga Deepak was the atomic resonance frequency ...

She discussed Ragas of Carnatic music with Savithri aunty. Some information that she got was all noted mentally, since the notepad only had Thirukkural specifics.

It seemed to her that six months of her life felt like 60 years of information getting processed, she wondered what had happened to her.

She heard the song playing '*Vathikkuchi pathikkaadhu da.. Yaarum vandhu orasara varailyile...*' Gautham was a big fan of Ajith Kumar, a Tamil actor, whose song was playing with Dweepa and Gautham dancing for it. She paid attention to the lyrics and it occurred to her.

Selvy shook... She frantically searched her pocket for the notepad... And wrote... *Yaarum vandhu orasara varayilla...* It won't ignite until something strikes it...Adhigaram-Poraiudaimai = P++

CHAPTER FIFTEEN

# Rajam, the Numismatist

Chennai.

It was time for Selvy, Yegna and Sendhan to leave. They had been in Aralvaimozhi for one week. Selvy had to visit Chennai too. Selvy had grown inquisitive about history all of a sudden and wanted to see the coin collection of her *paati*. Though at the back of her head, she was telling herself that she shouldn't underestimate her family, they weren't those naive relatives that she saw at home, humble and simple. She had imagined Rajam *paati*'s hobby was collecting coins. And she imagined seeing some album, larger than a school project. Probably a set of folders with coins stuck on them.

Rajam Paati's house was a beautiful independent house built in the 1970s, featuring a Madras ceiling and two-foot-wide walls. It is in Raja Annamalaipuram, near Mylapore. Today, this type of house would be referred to as a bungalow. From the gate a passageway with flower gardens on either side lead to a portico with pillars on both sides. The entrance door was a 10 feet tall, teak door. There were three long steps to the entrance door, that extended between the wide pillars on either side of the door. On one end there was also a slope. Great grandmom had been wheel chair bound after an age, and this alteration which was made with cement, was done exclusively for her it seems. On either side of this were two platforms for sitting. The entrance was beautifully decorated. It had red oxide and Athangudi tiles.

On the lower level, there was a large living room, a big kitchen, a prayer room, and the bedroom of her grandparents. On the upper level, there is a room for Amma and Appa, a room for aunty, and two additional bedrooms. On the right side of the house, there was space for parking a car, and on the left side, in a small area, was their pet dog Subramani. At the back of the house, there was an outhouse that had grandfather's clinic. There was a room on the upper level of the outhouse as well. But Selvy never ventured to see what was in the outhouse. From 5 PM, several patients came to see the *thatha*. The clinic was open till 9 PM. A few chairs were set up outiside the clinic, in the parking lot. Mani *Anna* and Dhana *Akka* efficiently took care of managing the patients and arranging medicines for them, through the small pharmacy which had Siddha medicines.

Selvi, Senthan, and Yegna arrived at Rajam *Paati*'s house, took a bath, and got ready to have breakfast. The assembled at a dining table, which was adorned with beautiful wooden carvings and located behind the reception area, the grandmother and Yegna serve Pongal, Dosa, peanut chutney, and sambar to Selvy, Sendhan and *Thatha*.

Rajam took Selvy to the room on the first floor of the outhouse behind their main house, immediately after breakfast. She was as excited as a kid waiting to show her stuff to her friend. There were huge cupboards with glass doors and over 20 cabinets, it was nothing less than a museum of sorts. It was nothing like the one Selvy had imagined. In each one, there were several drawers. Above each cabinet, a time period was indicated. On the wall, there was a framed certificate. It was a certificate awarded for India's finest private coin collection. It had been issued by the Central Archaeological Research Institute. Selvy cringed and wanted to hide her face in shame because she neither had a clue about her ancestry, nor about the elders in the family. Her mother, *chiththi*, grandmothers etc stood tall as the village deities, *Veli kaatha Maariyamman* idols, she saw on her way back.

During her college days, even though she stayed at her grandmother's house, she had never seen this room until that day. With school and tuition classes, a long line of patients downstairs, she recalled thinking how she didn't want to waste time talking to anyone. All these thoughts came to her mind, and Selvi felt a rush of guilt.

Rajam Paati opened a cupboard, and pulled a drawer with trays. In every tray, there were 50 coins, neatly arranged, with cotton spread under them, and a numbered slip placed on top of each stack. On the other side of the room, there was another smaller cupboard with the details of each number in the catalogue. It was as professionally organised as a library or a museum. Shock upon shock awaited the one who thought the coins were merely collected as an amused school child. There were three cabinets labelled BC.

Yegna entered the room with a flask of coffee. On a table near the entrance of the room, she placed a flask and some tumblers, then approached Rajam and secretly asked, "*Amma*, should we mention that coin?" Rajam had already examined it and knew that it was not a coin but a piece of stone that was significant in another sense. She gestured to show it later.

Rajam showed a carved coin of *Vinayakar, the elephant God,* from the 3rd to 4th century BCE. She mentioned that it belonged to the time of the Kushanas, and underlined that it was not a usual find, and was a precious one in her collection. Although *Vinayakar* was greatly celebrated by North Indians, she said that this ancient coin was found at Vathaapi. Yegna whispered, "*Vaathaapi Ganapathim bhaje hum...*"

Rajam opened a safety locker. Inside which were some gold coins. Holding two coins in her hand, she asked Selvi, "Can you figure out which one is pure gold and which one is gold-plated?"

Selvi, was shocked and she sat in silence. She was first in shock that the con collection was this huge, now she was more shocked to see a gold coin, that too an ancient one! Rajam pointed to a coin bearing the image of King Henry. "They had tried a crude gold plating technique on these copper coins," Rajam said, explaining how this coin demonstrated the king's conspiracy. "He didn't wish gold coins to be at the disposal of common people and therefore had plated copper coins for circulation. However, the nose which was protuding in the coins, showed the copper underneath as the coins were used extensively, the gold plating had worn off. People mocked the king, calling him 'Copper Nose Henry', which was recorded in European history." She further shared that these coins had made their way across the sea to merchants here, and one had gotten into Rajam's Paati's collection too.

She picked up another box. Inside were gold coins bearing Tamil inscriptions that Selvi could understand. She explained that these dated back to the Chola and Pandya kings and described how each king had engraved different symbols. After securely putting all the coins in boxes and locking them, Rajam sat in a chair near the table, while Selvy and Yegna sat on the window sill which had been converted to a seating platform, and enjoyed their coffee.

As they relished their coffee, *Paati* shared, "What you saw just now wasn't pure gold coins as well!" Selvy spilt her drink in shock. She asked, "What, *Paati*, were our kings involved in such dishonest means as well? The coins seemed so flawless!"

Rajam *Paati* revealed a significant historical truth. "Gold was not highly valued in our country. We exported iron from our land in exchange for gold. Any kind of gold coins that people had here primarily came in through foreign trade. Barter was the usual practice within our country," she said. Selvi asked, "Then, are copper coins too, are they?" Rajam *Paati* replied, "No, dear, these are gold coins that have been artificially altered through a process... that of 'Alchemical transmutation'. In any laboratory test, if one examined, they would be identified as gold. However, ancient medicinal texts mention certain herbs that can be used to distinguish between this and real gold. This is not real gold."

Selvi exclaimed, "Can I take a look at them again!"

As the two of them went back to look at the boxes, Yegna, with a smile, took the tumblers and the flask and went downstairs.

"I don't know if I can show you everything in just one day. But there is one important box you must see," said Rajam *Paati*.

Taking out a gold coin from a box, she said, "This one is special. A *Tantri* (a practitioner of occult traditions) near our hometown made this. I was born and raised in Kanyakumari. There, it was a tradition for both families to bring gold coins during engagements to finalize the alliance. A woman next door did not have the money for this ceremony. They were poor so they came to our house and borrowed some copper coins. First, they gave it to a *Tantri* from another town to try and trasmutate it to gold, but it didn't work out". He told them to try again after one *mandalam*.

Selvy interrupted and asked, "What is a *mandalam*?".

"A *mandalam* is 41 days," she replied and added, "Some say it is 45 days, and others say 48 days. Even modern mental health practitioners emphasize the significance of such time calculations. They say that if you consistently do something for 21 days, it becomes a habit. If you do something for 45 days, it becomes a part of your being. For practices like meditation, if you start with 9 uninterrupted days, followed by 21 days, and then continue for 45, it becomes an integral part of your daily routine, just like brushing your teeth or bathing," she explained.

For a moment, Selvi thought about how like waves crashed into one another, her grandmother, could speak with newfound enthusiasm about any topic. She was like an ocean of knowledge—a deep ocean where what she was currently experiencing was barely ripples which were wetting her feet at the beach. A big treasure trove of knowledge would be burried deep within her too.

"Let me get to the story of the 'corrupted currency'," she said. "That trickster *Tantri* was a fraud. This is the money he made. The groom's family called off the engagement after learning about the fake coins given by the bride's family. However, at another sister's (who lived in another street) house, they did the same thing with another *Tantri* and exchanged 101 copper coins, borrowed from us and transmutated the coins successfully to gold, resulting in a marriage being arranged. They handed over one coin, along with the invitation, to the grandfather when they came to invite them for the wedding. This is that one. To date, not a single machine has been invented to distinguish between an actual gold coin and this alchemically transmutated one," she said.

"*Paati*, did *Kollu thatha*( great grandfather) give a lot of money for your wedding too?" Selvi asked. "Oh, you naughty little brat... My father was someone who valued education. He was very keen that I should study. I didn't even have a groom lined up, since I was more educated than many in the village. Then came your grandfather, who promised that he would ensure I would continue my studies. He made my mother understand that we would not have any children until I completed my degree and made her understand that it was better for me to be allowed to stay at their house itself till then. His parents were also people with such a big heart. I am indeed lucky. My mother-in-law took care of me as if i were her own daughter. An angel of a woman." she said, her eyes brimming with emotion.

Grandpa studied Siddha medicine (the South Indian medical field) and later worked as a professor at a Government Siddha college before retiring. Selvy felt proud of her grandfather.

Selvy went around all the cupboards with Rajam, listening to stories, and she felt as if she had traveled to another world.

"When your mother is here, I get so much time for myself and for things I am passionate about. I am blessed to have a great mother-in-law and an even better daughter-in-law! She handles all my work whenever she comes. She's such a lovely girl. She completely takes care of everything in the kitchen, she must have cooked something wonderful," said *Paati*, and the two came downstairs after a hearty time.

Just as *Paati* mentioned, Yegna had prepared a six-course feast and arranged it beautifully on the table. Senthan and Grandpa were playing with Subramani, the Rajapalayam dog. After everyone joined, they sat together for lunch and chatted heartily, recalling Selvy's bloopers during her stay with her grandparents.

Selvy was taking notes in her diary, after lunch. She was too overwhelmed to sleep after the morning exercise. It was while writing about the coins that underwent the alchemical transmutation that Selvy understood why Valli *chitthi* had asked her to meet *Paati*. She also understood the profound truth behind the experiment Valli had conducted earlier in their school, everything dawned on her. For a moment, her eyes welled up. She thought to herself, "I am conducting experiments in a foreign land, unaware of the treasures lying in my own backyard... This is a real test that is unfolding in my life," and she felt a wave of emotion.

Around 6 o'clock, Rajam *Paati* lit a lamp in her prayer room and began her worship. She was a *SriVidya upasaka* (practiotioner of a special religious ritual practised by a cult which follows worship of Goddess Shakthi) . It was Annapoorani *mami* from the neighboring house who had introduced her to this cult. Rajam woke up at 4 every morning and performed her prayers for two hours. Her prayer hall was neatly arranged. It had many curious artefacts.

Yegna and Anandhan were not religious, and there wasn't even a room like this in Selvy's house. Therefore, Selvy observed everything keenly. Near the lamp, there was a *kolam (*a pattern drawn with rice flour). It resembled some shapes etched on the floor of the Alchemical museum at Prague. Selvy eagerly asked, "What is this?". Paati's voice responded,"This is called the *Navagraha kolam*. We draw a different pattern for every day of the week".

Immediately, Selvi asked, "Does Navagraha mean 9 planets, *Paati*?" Rajam *Paati* smiled thinking to herself, look at her asking how her dad did... "Since we are living on the Earth, when we mention the 9 planets in astrology, it can't refer to 9 planets, since we have to exclude this planet. It refers to those celestial bodies that have the power to influence the Earth with their magnetic field. These are the *Navagrahas*. In the solar system, we consider planets only up to Saturn, so how many would that be?"

Selvy promptly said "Five, excluding Earth."

"Exactly! Five planets, which means Mercury, Venus, Mars, Jupiter, and Saturn. Now along with these we consider the Sun, Moon, Rahu, and Ketu as celestial bodies which can influence the magetic field of Earth. These are the 9 *Grahas*. Rahu and Ketu are not planets; they are like a magnetic field lines that surrounds each planet. You have studied about magnets, haven't you?" she asked.

"*Paati*, my field involves electromagnetic forces," Selvy replied.

"Rahu and Ketu are the points of intersection of the magnetic field lines meet between the Sun, Moon, and Earth. Rahu is in the north of Earth's equator, while Ketu is in the south. Imagine them like the strings around the churner of a yogurt pot, which are pulled to churn it." she explained.

Rajam *Paati* said, "Your grandfather will tell you more stories about how the nine planets would influence animals, plants, and trees."

Selvy asked, " like what?"

*Paati* said, "I'll tell you just one example. It seems pearls are formed within an oyster when a particular star shines in the sky. *Thatha* knows many more such interesting things" .

Selvy turned to Yegna and asked, " *Amma*, do you know to draw *kolams*?"

Rajam *Paati* and Yegna looked at each other and laughed, saying, "Every time you all come here, it's your mother who makes the *kolam*. She also makes it at the entrance. Have you never noticed that even once?" Selvi stood there, astonished, thinking about how self-centered she had been in her life, completely unaware of those around her.

"I'm really sorry, *Ma*. I haven't paid attention to it until now" She said as she hugged her mother. Yegna, still laughing, commented, "If your aunt had made it, you and Dweepa would have contributed as well. You know how much assistance little Senthan has provided!"

Selvi replied,"I thought you don't believe in traditions and scriptures, so I assumed!?'

Yegna then explained, "There's no connection between the two. What I don't follow are mindless practices. This is a scientifically based practice. When women bend down and draw *kolams*, blood flows to their head. It's an important exercise for being vigilant throughout the day and for multitasking. When you wake up and the rising sun's rays hit your spine, vitamin D is synthesized, which strengthens the bones. The *kolam* powder contains granules of fine sand. The nerve endings at the fingertips stimulated by these which activate the right lobe of the brain. The *kolam* itself is a symmetrical pattern. In other words, this *Navagraha kolam* is designed like a cymatic pattern of the radio signals emitted from each planet," Yegna overwhelmed Selvy with information just to show off that she wasn't this unassuming glorified maid servant of the family.

"Amma, then it seems as if I am the most ignorant one in this family. Each of you give me TED talks, my God!" Selvy remarked."

After playing cricket with friends on the street, Sendan came in through the rear entrance and hugged his grandmother. She embraced him and sang a famous song about how Lord Krishna used to playfully tease his *Gopis*, adding her own lines, *'Pinnalai pinnindrizhuththaan sendhan paatiyai pinindru katti anaiththaan*'. He pulled my braid from behind me, Sendhan hid behind me and embraced me stealthily.

"It's already 6:30. We need to go to the temple and mark attendance with Kabali," she said as if it was a school.

Selvi replied, "I wish to join you too."

The grandmother and granddaughter got into the auto rickshaw driven by their regular driver, Annadurai *Anna*. "That's *thatha*'s auto. An arrangement of kindness by thatha to help his old friend's son, Annadurai *Anna*. He drives the auto everyday from 7:30 AM. He picks up children, who have to be dropped off at school, then drives other passengers till 5:30 PM. By which time he drops off the children back to their homes too, comes to pick up *Paati* for her Temple visit. He then leaves the auto in the house, hands over the keys to thatha and goes home. He comes whenever they need him and takes them wherever they wished to go and earns through the fares he drives otherwise. Even though thatha has a car, *Paati* feels claustrophobic and gets motion sickness in it. So to most places *Paati* travels by auto. Sendhan shared these while both were waiting for Auto anna to arrive.

"Paati, won't you get tired? Your day seems to start at 3:00 AM. I hardly see you sit idle through the day!" asked Selvy.

Paati smilingly replied, " I do take a power nap in the afternoon for an hour. Besides I sleep at 9:30. I guess that is more than enough to recharge my batteries"

"Paati, I have a few questions, some may be offensive. Would you mind my asking?" asked Selvy as politely as she could.

"Shoot them darling", said Paati.

"How is it that you seem to accept idol worship? What is your opinion about the war between languages and their antiquity, which language between Tamil and Sanskrit do you think is older? Do you think the Puranas or other mythological tales have secret codes or decknamens hidden in them?" She asked all of it as if releasing steam from a pressure cooker.

By that time, the auto reached the temple. Paati told Selvy that they could go in and continue discussing. On her way in, the lady who was stringing flowers, the uncle who had a shop with items required for pooja, many who met her regularly, greeted her. She walked straight to the small temple for Lord Ganesh inside the Temple complex. she did 11 thoppukkaranams( an exercise that is popular in the west in the name of super brain yoga, where one holds the ear lobes, and does a squat) and called Selvy. They began walking. She pointed to a lingam painted on the ceiling of the mandapam on the left. She said, as we walk, you would notice that the long part of the lingam would face us all the time. Let us talk after the darshan, she said and devotedly walked towards the sanctum sanctorum.

Selvy imagined Kapaleeswarar sitting with a register, marking her attendance. 'Rajam...' called Kapaleeswarar and 'Ullen ayya'(Present Sir) answered Rajam. Selvy chuckled at the imagination but quietly walked right beind Paati, without disturbing her ritualistic pauses at various deities around, or gestures of prayer. From the thoppukkaranam at the Ganesha temple, to clapping and saying, please let Lord Shiva know I was here, at a place which was labelled, chandikeswara( believed to be a book keeper of Lord Shiva), literally marking her attendance, taking drops of water dripping from a vent (that was the outlet through which the water poured over the deity came out) and sprinkling it on her head, then consuming the water given by the priest with a half squat and then running her wet hands over her eyes, etc.

After visiting both the deities of the temple, Karpagambal and Kapaleeswarar, the duo completed one circumambulation and reached the mandapam again and sat down. While walking around, she had been thinking about the lingam that seemed to turn with one and then had observed that it was drawn on an oval and understood that an ellipse has two foci. On one, they could have painted the lingam and extended the spout till the second focal point, to create this illusion. She had another doubt that could be a possible explanation for some other spiritual symbolism. She made a mental note of it.

She began her questions with, "Paati, why must one come to the temple, when God is omnipresent?"

Paati smiled and said" This was exactly what your dad asked. Well, I haven't been able to convince him with this answer, he doesnt visit temples. Let me see how you take this. If you take all the mantras we recite, be it in any language, don't you think they are affirmations? If one went to a therapist and they suggested to tell oneself, a ho'oponopono prayer, that is considered trendy. But here, you recite it to resonate with many other who are there and the resonance makes it work manifold for everyone. Let me simplify this. In a class, if you have achieved something, How would it be if your teacher appreciated you, versus, the whole class or say the whole school applauding you. which is more effective in making it feel like an achievement? Praying at home with using only your energy versus using the divine manifestation capabilities of everyone around is analogous to the example. Mind you, in the temple, you are contributing your power for the manifestation of dreams of others as well, which also adds a positive Karmic impact."

"Some westerners felt is it disgusting to worship the lingam. they felt it reminded them of the male sex organ and the female one in fusion. But this doesn't say anything about our ancient people. this shows the perversion of the observer. According to me this is a form that is geometrically convenient in many ways. If there was something that fell from the ceiling, it would just slip and fall. Vibrations would rebound. Our positive thought would be amplified by its reflection in all directions. Have you tried crushing an egg by pressing it between your fingers? It is impossible. The Lingam is that kind of a symbolism. "

"Another thing I strongly believe is that temples were not just places of worship. They had healers living here. The main lingam or in some temples like Palani, the deity Murugan's statue was made using herbal transmutation of alloys. It had nine types of poisonous substances called the Navapashaanam. These seem to have healing properties. The water poured over the deity is in a way a procedure called serial dilution that is the practice in Homeopathy. They considered this water sacred, as a religious ritual and it was able to cure diseases without stating. The water that is given here to drink, has herbs like Tulsi, an antiseptic, and spices like cardomom and some natural camphor added. There are capable of curing many diseases of the gut and indirectly improve health. A temple is like a multispeciality clinic." she said.

Selvi felt intimidated by the height of pilosophical wisdom each of the elders in her family were. She had only considered the qualified ones like her dad, her grandfathers etc as great so far. Now the women were just putting her ego to shame. She asked," Paati, how could alchemical experiments be carried out in the temple? Wasn't a lab required for them?"

Paati continued, "Have you heard of Devadasis? I always felt they had been diagnostic assistants."

Selvy excalimed in shock. "What are you saying?"

"Look at the colourful gopuram. Here, take these binoculars." said Paati. It seemed like Rajam was also very well prepared for this KT(Knowledge transfer) exercise. " Let me know if you found something interesting" She added.

"Paati, does Lord Shiva play the veena?" asked Selvy.

"Baley" said Paati with a pride as if acknowleding Selvy's keen observation. "You were able to spot that because you have always been seeking things that were out of the ordinary. Each person looks at things that are aligned to their quest. For example, someone who is interested in animal welfare would have observed all the types of creatures on the gopuram. The Devadasis, with their dance movements, could have indicated the specific problems of each of the devotees who come in, to the archagar or the priest, who suggested them to follow a ritualistic prayer specific and personalised to each. For some it was to try pouring water over the deity and use the water. For some it was lighting lamps, etc. These were also based on the astrological signs that the devotees belonged to. Since astrology has been known to be completely unique for every individual. I know you might question that too. But broadly, think of a person born in the winter months, and their preferences and one born in the Summer. They would be different right. It is similar to that." Paati said.

Eventhough it was overwhelming information, Selvy had developed the apetite to digest and assimilate everything, since the fire under her belly, about finding the wisdom hidden or coded had been lit by Anandavalli chiththi.

Selvy asked, " Paati do you think these are specific to religions?"

Paati said, " Before religions emerged, people worshiped nature. The pyramids, the Kaaba of Mecca, the Churches, all of them do things beyond rituals. There is a sense of togetherness as humans, a feeling of oneness beyond differences, selfish desires or wants, and as long as we keep that as the pillar of a place of worship, I guess the purpose of every religion would be achieved. When many humans come together with that single minded devotion, there is no way for any force of nature, whichever name you wish to address it as, God or Universal energy or whatever... to escape but to show its Divine Grace. Every religion emerged in a time when people were hopeless, troubled, and had sought divine intervention. Every religious leader, saint or prophet, had emerged to give humans hope and to guide them through a path where they could handle challenges of life.

Rajam Paati, was now distracted with many people begining to approach her with their How are you-s. Selvy knew they were curious to see me too. She introduced Selvy proudly as a scientist at CERN.

Rajam and Selvy sat with eyes closed for a few minutes. Selvy wanted this for just sorting all the information she had been introduced to, from her

RAM into Long term memory. She heard Nikola Tesla's words. Everything in the Universe is energy, frequency and vibration. A light, travelled like a strand from under the feet of people circumambulating the temple, and flowed towards the sanctum sanctorum. From beneath the lingam in the sanctum, an entangled mass of energies shining as a bright rope now shot upwards. She was now looking from a drone's perspective at the temple. That beam of light was directed towards the sky, merging with the radiant light flowing from many nearby temples and places of worship, enveloping everything like the ozone layer that protects the world.

Suddenly awakened by the sound of a bell, she opened her eyes. Religion was created to provide humans with guidance and faith in life. This was its true purpose. She thought that in today's context, due to some people not aligning correctly with that purpose, many issues had arisen. Rajam *Paati* approached and said, "Let's do this, darling." She immediately stood up. *Paati* handed her a round stone wrapped in a yellow cloth from her flower basket. Selvy understood it to be a baton given to her for the relay race. Looking upwards, she thought, "I must do this responsibly, O Universe..." The light beam sparkled like a diamond halo...

CHAPTER SIXTEEN

# Women's Day, 2022

Geneva

Meena organised something again. She wanted the young women of CERN to take part in a series of videos, and she was planning to use that to motivate children and young adults from all over the world. Meena, Selvy felt, was such an enterprising person, probably because of the fire in her to re-establish her Pataliputra's pride.

Selvy sometimes felt she wasn't so. In fact, she was now at number 18. She had done 16 and 17 before 15, and yesterday she cracked *Adhigaram* 15 too. And she knew what the greatness of Thirukkural was and what level of encryption had gone into the entire text. It has stayed for so long unnoticed, right under everyone's nose.

Selvy felt, so true, if you wish to stay unnoticed, don't hide where no one can find, disguise, and stay with the crowd. That's how things had to be. And she also felt instead of the so-called competition between labs like today, labs of the past were collaborating. They probably traded information for ores. That's the gemstone wealth. What are gemstones after all, organised crystals which can be analysed? Used as Prisms, filters of Electromagnetic radiations, even particle capturing targets.

Even today, the richest countries in terms of Natural wealth are the most economically backward. In fact, the moment this realisation dawns, those who are sucking them would have to succumb.

As Meena's bestie, Selvy had to do all the odd jobs like holding the camera, lights, microphone, etc, editing the videos and putting them together. Writing the description for the video, etc.

Selvy was happy to help, but she was preoccupied with the connection of gossip with nobility. The thought of gossip reminded her of the party the previous day.

She suddenly remembered Dweepa's colleague, Branka. Until Women's Day celebrations were over, she wasn't planning any serious work. She felt like making a quick visit to Dweepa's place and connecting with Branka.

Dweepa, Branka and Selvy sat down with their cups of coffee. Selvy asked Branka about internet routers, chips used in them, if there was any exclusive element in them, etc. Branka explained in great detail. She was an Electronics engineer. Selvy didn't want to share her work with Branka.

She had run out of things she wanted to talk about. Dweepa and Branka were playing with Aakash and began gossiping about people in their office.

Selvy thought she would share Lenka's cousin's story and about the Beauty pageant. But Selvy realised it was completely unnecessary, utterly ignoble.

That's it... That's the connection then...

She needed one more proof. Branka was talking about her child's birthday party. She had a son too, 3 years old. They had some Helium balloons and had fun with it.

Selvy wondered what would happen if you inhaled other Noble gases and how would the pitch be. She quietly escaped the gossip that wasn't even remotely connected to her, and she browsed YouTube. There was a video. And she got her answer. Eureka moment...

She scribbled a lot of things this time on the notepad and felt she would begin letting everyone know her name. She wouldn't call herself Selena anymore. Thiruniraiselvy was bloating with pride and the brilliance of Valluvar.

If this is 18, then 19 and 20 are cups of cakes, she felt. So easy...

CHAPTER SEVENTEEN

# Thoothukkudi Jeyaraman

Selvy, Sandy and Yegna were getting ready to leave. Anandan had joined the Chennai office. Yegna had to go back to Delhi and shift again. But this time they could stay with *Paati, thatha*. There was the portion on the first floor, which *Paati* kept clean and neat for her son and daughter to stay.

Selvy went to the terrace to meet *thatha*. He maintained a herbal garden on the terrace where there were vegetables enough for the family too. She knew *thatha* was very fond of plants.

She had spent most of her time studying on the terrace when she was here. As soon as she went up to her favourite spot there, she remembered, 'Wurtz reaction, Markovnikov's addition, Mensuration, Matrices and all the topics of class 12' as if they were rippling back to her from the space, the veLi.

Selvy noticed that *thatha* was growing rows of *methi*, fenugreek plants. She didn't know what he was up to.

Sendhan called out to Selvy and *thatha* and they both went down.

Bala *paati's* student Thoothukudi Jeyaraman had come. Valli *chiththi* had sent him to meet Selvy and hand her two sheets of paper. It seemed as if Rajam *paati* and Narayanan *thatha* knew about it.

Anandan and Yegna were busy discussing packers and movers. Sendhan went out to meet his new friends.

Jeyarama, take the coffee, she said with fondness. She enquired about his hostel and asked him to stay till dinner. She affectionately said he should take a sleeper bus. And that the push back seats weren't comfortable for this much distance.

Selvy realised he had travelled by bus to reach here. She didn't know what to expect.

With the arrogance and attitude of a city bred, particle physics research student working at CERN, she asked, "so you studied BA Tamil, is it?"

Jeyaraman was calm. He said he was a Ph.d student. He was unassumingly timid, Puny and looked malnourished. He was wearing oversized clothes. Selvy noticed that he had the three circles tattooed on his arm. It was a crude country tattoo. He had a folder just like Valli. It was, in fact, the one that Valli had.

Selvy immediately realised that she had made a mistake. She changed her body language and said, *sollunga anna.*

Jeyaraman said Bala amma was his research guide's guide and that he was working on the Keezhadi project as an archaeologist.

Rajam added that some coins in the backyard were his collection. Her Coin collection was registered with the ASI, Archaeological Society of India. And since he travelled so much, he needed a place. He couldn't keep it in the University or in his hostel.

He asked if Selvy had some research experience.

Selvy felt her ego was questioned now. She boasted about her summer research fellowships. She also proudly shared about a book Dweepa and Selvy published through an online publishing platform. It was the compilation of their coded letters to each other and a guide to encrypting information.

Jeyaraman smiled calmly. He took only one sheet and gave it to her to try decoding.

It said *Aathichudi* and had the twelve vowels of Tamil. The letters were numbered.

Selvy didn't know what to do.

He said, " The clue is *Aathichudi.*"

She was extremely confused. She had to surrender.

Jeyaraman said. "*Aathichudi* had two verses that were for you to decode."

Selvy was struggling to recall *Aathichudi.*

Jeyaraman took the paper that Valli and Selvy wrote on at Poigai dam from his folder and handed it to her.

She could still not decipher it.

He then explained that *enn ezhuthu igazhel* was the 7th alphabet and *othuvadhu ozhiyel* was the 11th. He then said ஃ was the symbol of God. *Agathiya muni* had 12 disciples, representing the 12 *uyir ezhuthukkal* (vowels).

This *Avvayar* was the disciple of the last disciple of the 7th disciple of *Agathiyar.*The code that reveals this is based on a vedic coding system. They call it '*Katapayadhi*'.

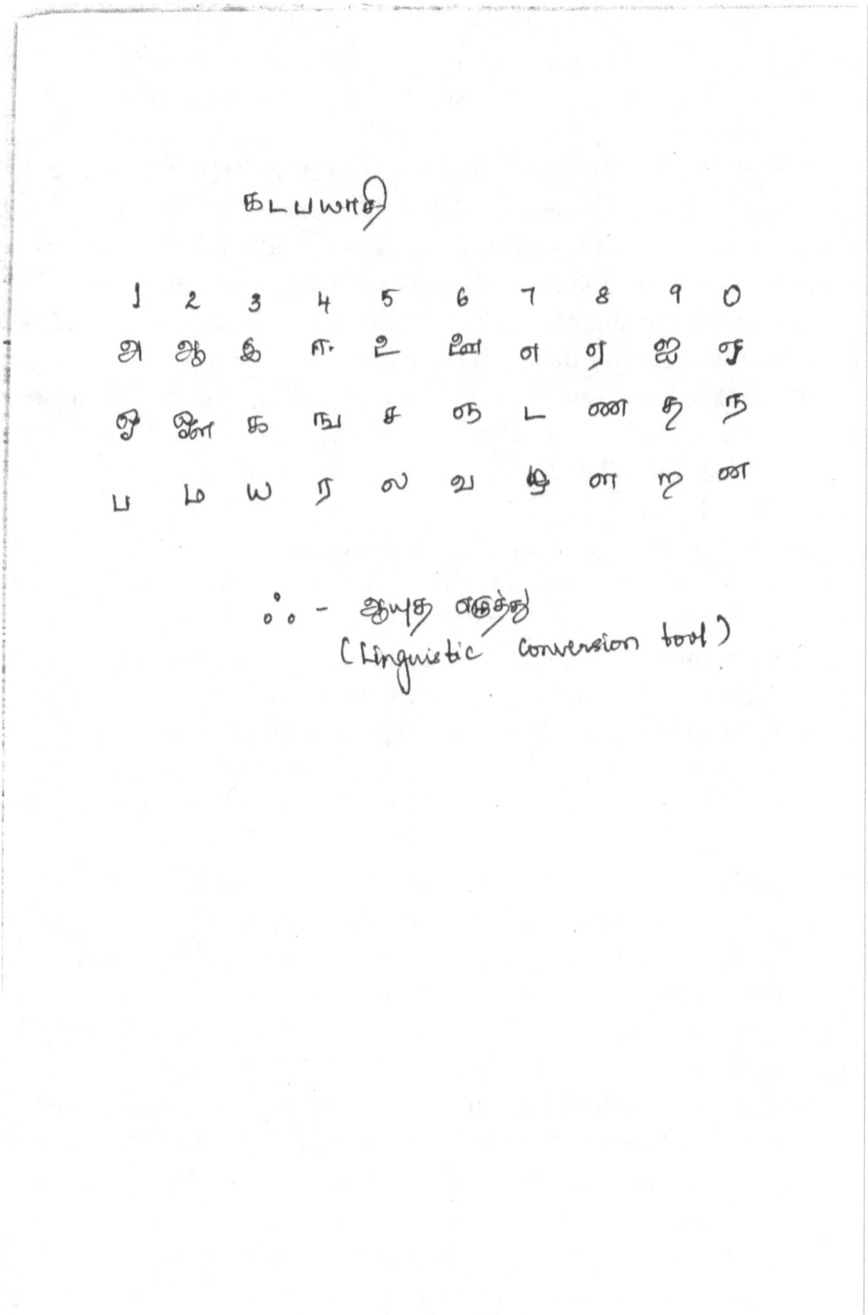

கடபயாதி

| 1 | 2 | 3 | 4 | 5 | 6 | 7 | 8 | 9 | 0 |
|---|---|---|---|---|---|---|---|---|---|
| அ | ஆ | இ | ஈ | உ | ஊ | எ | ஏ | ஐ | ஒ |
| ஓ | ஔ | க | ங | ச | ஞ | ட | ண | த | ந |
| ப | ம | ய | ர | ல | வ | ழ | ள | ற | ன |

ஃ - ஆயுத எழுத்து
(Linguistic conversion tool)

Enter Caption

He asked her if she knew about the *Gurukulam* system. She vaguely recalled something her dad told her once about the caste system and its connection. She safely said no, instead of getting another stare for acting like a 'know-it-all.

He said, "for ease of understanding, my code would be 145. He handed her a paper with the *katapayadhi* system. My name's starting letter is 'J", in Tamil it would start with "Cha" and its number code is (5), my *guru* 's name is Ramachandran (4) and his *guru*, Bala (1)." Selvy now understood.

He said, "the period before the Sangam had a casteless land. The *Manu needhi* was written back then, and for that society.

The land masses were divided into 32 linguistic regions. These were based on the 32 cardinal directions, with Ujjain as the centre. The languages in that period were all oral, without scripts. The languages, however, were all considered equal.

Just like today, anyone who wants to do higher studies can travel to any land to learn their field of expertise. A conversion matrix that says the alphabet phonics in each region is available in every region. Instead of having one language that all had to learn, like the English language today, they had their language with the phonic conversion matrix.

Yegna pitched in to explain, One minute *thambi,* I'll explain this and go back. Some of the root words between languages in South India are the same, only the phonics differ. So in Tamil, we say 'Paal' for milk, and in Karnataka they say 'Haalu'. Effectively the replacement is like the Ctrl H function, find 'Pa' replace with'Ha'. and end the word with an 'oo' sound

Thankfully, all this was taught orally. The Tamil matrix has been either lost with the *Kumari Kandam*'s sinking or has been codified in some text. That is yet to be established. But the Brahmins were instructed after the Gupta period to keep the oral tradition of *Veda abhyasam* and is taught for those who learn Rig Veda.

There was transparency of knowledge transfer, and anyone could go anywhere to learn any skill. That is why there are linguistic trails all around for any language you consider. If the language had been one of the parent languages, it would be traceable.

The *Gurukula* system expects the equivalent of a transfer of adoption right to the Guru that the person joins."

Selvy was doubtful. She asked, " are you sure of this?"

Jeyaraman said, "Have you read '*Amar chitra Katha*'? You might have seen that Vishwamitra was a son of a king who learnt to become a brahmin. Even Vasishta was so called *Shudhra* who learned to become a brahmin. They say they were *guna brahmanas* and *kula kshatriyas* and *Shudhras*. Similarly, Veda Vyasar who compiled the Vedas into the form it is in today was born to a *rishi* and a fisher woman. Parasuraman was born to a sage, but he was a skilled *kshatriya* (a *brahmana kula kshatriya*), Chanakya was a political strategist, and so on. Even women were warriors, Sita, Kaikeyi etc. The learned Avvayar (etymologically which could indicate she was a minister, '*avai*' means congregation) is one in tamil. The Rig Veda has chapters written by Rishikas. Thus the Gurukulams had many such learned people with diverse expertise.

The Guptas have their own secrets. Think of what Gupta means in Hindi. 'Secret'. The puranas which were stories added after Gupta period, have numerous coded things. There are also mythological stories where there are logical gaps, these are our targets for decoding. All these evidences point towards the equal society of the past. Now if you ask about whether these are facts or fiction, that is left to oneself. but there cannot be so many coincidences that point to existence of such a civilised society in the past.

The Tamil brahmi script has 'ஃ' getting out of the list of *uyir ezhuthukkal* and there was an alphabet symbol introduced in its place for 'e'. So, seems like Guptas had a United Nations of that time and took some decisions after their war and after Chandra Gupta Maurya renounced everything and became a monk." They could have decided to safeguard secrets in the army as harmless stories which would be kept alive as folklore. those who wished to study deeply, were revealed in due time.

He continued after checking if Selvy was listening, "The 32 cardinal directions were open for anyone to move anywhere. But think of who would usually travel everywhere. In today's world too, political leaders, businessmen, traders, and scholars are the group of people who travel. Sometimes chosen people travel for learning military strategies or for getting trained in some specific skill in some particular place. Thus, people who were agriculturists, or artisans or those who worked at a place for long periods of time never moved.

The *gurukulam* was like the modern-day University, not the modern-day school. There were departments of specialization for every field. Within two years, the teachers were able to judge the abilities of a child. And just like in higher education, you learn two languages in addition to the specific skill, there was a local language and a general language, along with the skill set. But the general language was optional and only those who travelled learnt it. It is not clear what that common language was. Those who learnt that general language would also know the local language of a region they belonged to.

The directions among the 32 which were located in cooler places were facing fertility issues which resulted in the mothers refusing to part with their babies, or some natural calamity separated the land masses and some *gurukulams* had ceased to exist. The people then started invading lands. If you think carefully, those people who go to another land and invade, either come from places where food was scarce, or resources were limited for livelihood.

Similar to the modern day British invaders and their strategy to divide and rule that they practised in India and influenced the minds of people saying, thinkers and businessmen, who travel are superior and knowledgeable, and that people who do laborious work were inferior, during the Gupta period, the *manu needhi* was twisted into *Manusmriti* ( translated as what they recalled from memory of the *Manu needhi*) to make Brahmins believe they were superior in some way. The dignity of labour was diluted. Eventually, the system became more selfish, where the caste system became converted to one that was based on birth and not skill."

Selvy felt honoured to meet such a knowledgeable Jeyaraman. Selvy thought to herself, she never knew what caste she belonged to.

She asked Jeyaraman, "Sanskrit was the oldest language, isn't it? That's what she learnt all along in her school days."

Jeyaraman jerked in offence. He said the Vedas were in another dialect different from the present-day form of Sanskrit. The modern-day Sanskrit is a mixture of Pali, Prakrut, and some Dravidian languages.

Selvy recalled that Sanskrit sounded like Tamil. The phonics of words ended with closing the mouth, like her teacher had taught. Like *pusthakam*, and not *pusthak* as in Hindi. She came back to this time and age after time-traveling with Jeyaraman.

"Now back to *Aathichudi*," said Jeyaraman.

The position of alphabet ஃ is indicative of the time of the text. If you look at Tamil scripts, the early scripts had a different way they were written, the symbol ஃ was used for the alphabet 'e' in the 6th century Tamil script. ஃ is a Decknamen. The Aathichudi has placed it at the end of the poem. So, the name of this Avvaiyar must begin with an alphabet under number 0, it could be 'o' or 'na'"he said.

"So, if you wrote something you would place at position 5, if your teacher wrote it would be in position 4 and Bala paati's work would have it in position 1. But your text would somewhere have the code 145 to indicate the guru lineage or the guru parampara, right?" asked Selvy. Jeyaraman was relieved that Selvy had understood now.

He then handed her the other sheet of paper.

It was a table with the chapters of the Thirukkural arranged in a very familiar fashion. She couldn't recognise it immediately. The boxes had the chapter names written inside. He said, Bala *amma* and Valli *Akka* feel you are right for this.

Selvy thought for a second, if this is the grand student of Bala *paati*, what level would she be at...

She also understood why the '*Guru Parampara-Parambarai*' was important and how the University students always mentioned the initials of their professors to mention which lab they were from, she recalled from one of her summer research fellowships, where they said, they were from Prof.NY's lab or NG's lab or DV's lab.

She felt she had been such a narrow-sighted person. Positive word for that is 'Focussed'. But reality is narrow knowledge. People all around her were storehouses.

He also handed her the Thirukkural written in spoken Tamil of this era. A book that he had authored.

He said that he had written it mainly for people like Selvy, who hadn't studied Tamil formally and would be thoroughly confused with the detailed commentaries that are available.

He said, "I have only one request, as Bala *amma*'s student. Please don't record your thoughts and ideas and findings on the internet. Don't keep an online document. Please don't store it on a gadget. Write it on notepads as you decode."

He asked, "do you know shorthand?"

She said, "yes". She had learnt it from her dad, who had gone for typewriting and shorthand classes while he was young.

He said, "write everything in shorthand." This generation doesn't know the coding language of the 1960s. See, every few years, all generations find a code language to encrypt things. recall who learnt shorthand. They were hired as secretaries. Those who noted down the instructions of a boss and used it for making official communications in a unique formal language."

We can discuss everything on your next visit.

He took blessings of Rajam *Paati*, and *thatha*. *Paati* had packed his dinner. Thatha gave him a bag of new clothes.

He said, "nalla saapdu pa. Eat well dear boy." Anandan came and met Jeyaraman and enquired affectionately.

He said, "hostel fees *ku vechukko thambi*, and gave him an envelope. For his hostel fees."

Selvy felt she was part of an army. It was as if she was in the quest of the holy grail. She felt extremely important and shivered at the responsibility everyone believes she can handle.

CHAPTER EIGHTEEN

# First Big Mistake

Geneva, March 9, 2022.

Selvy is extremely busy at the lab. She had spent evenings at Dweepa's place the last two days and was having quite a lot of work to complete. A conference was coming up. There was also the routine detector analysis that had to be done with utmost concentration. Her heart was swaying away from particle physics to Thirukkural. She had to focus.

Ida, from the water quality control department, came hurriedly. She said she needed to see the engineer urgently. Selvy was so glued to her work that she couldn't even process what Ida said.

She ran away after giving an enormous set of instructions.

Selvy had to literally turn her chair, close her eyes, and open it. She thought she would ask Ida to repeat whatever she said, but she was gone.

Ida was taking care of the quality of water that was getting into the cooling system and the water exiting the coolant. She usually is a calm person and never panics.

Selvy was clueless. Her tracker suddenly showed a peak, and she had to turn again to scrutinize the changes. She was detecting something intently and didn't see how much time had passed.

A group of Engineers came to her with Ida, and she asked her why Selvy had been so insensitive and mindless of how serious a matter like this was.

Ida ran away again.

Selvy didn't know what to do and panicked. She felt like crying, imagining all the worst-case scenarios, of a radiation leak, a pipeline leak at the inlet, which couldn't have happened since she would have known that showing up on her system. She imagined something going wrong with the coils because of the cooling system shutting off, somehow... Even the thought of someone committing suicide in the inlet or outlet sluices.

She started having a headache and suddenly blanked out.

Ida came in again and said that the problem was fixed. She said that she had needed help with calling the engineers. The cooling system had suddenly been shut.

Thankfully, they could fix it faster than she imagined. There was a leaky junction, which just needed replacement of a small washer. But since any leakage called for an SOS emergycy shutdown of the facility, the leak had triggered that. It was replaced within minutes and the colling system was restored. Ida was never this tense before. She was a warm person. She apologised to Selvy for all the unnecessary tension she was put into.

Selvy's heart began beating only after that moment. Ida said, "you looked as if you would pass out, girl. It wasn't that big a mistake. It wasn't your fault at all. Are you this scared of committing a mistake? You seem to be one who has never been pointed fingers at!"

Selvy said, it scared me to my bones.

Ida said, "drink some milk every day, don't lose all your energy worrying to your bones."

Selvy got it... She took her notepad again. It was *adhigaram* 21 now. 20 was easy. 21 terrified her to her 'bone'. She wasn't sure if there was that much knowledge or technology available back then. Nevertheless, noted down her suggestions for the connection.

She felt this was too big a connection and felt meeting Athai's husband, Shah Pappa, the Geologist, would be a good idea. She then remembered that they would have left for chennai. She kept that clarification for her trip.

CHAPTER NINETEEN

# Sendhan and 'Ayutha Ezhuthu' gang

Sendhan had become an activist after the *Jallikattu* protests. Though he wasn't in Chennai during 2016, only Selvy was. He had been looking for everything that would reveal the greatness of Tamil culture and he would write about it. He had a gang of friends in Chennai, which he had met through social media. They were the '*Ayutha ezhuthu*', meaning 'the alphabet.

Selvy felt she had to break the ice with her brother and bridge their gap. She herself had begun getting a lot interested in Tamil culture. She started the conversation by asking about the new song their gang came up with.

He got extremely happy and said that Yegna had written the song for them.

He started singing

Yaar mudhal ena aadhi manidhanai sadalathil thedum vaal arundha or mandhigal koottam...

உ

யார் முதல் என
ஆதிமனிதனை உடலத்தில் தேடும்
வால் அறுந்த வோர் மந்திகள் கூட்டம்

மறைகள் பிறந்தநாள் தொன்மையினில்
அதற்குமுன்னே தோன்றி திகழ்ந்தது எங்கள் நாகரிகம்

அன்றோ கண்டங்கள் தாண்டி நம் புகழ் ஓங்கிநின்றும்
வெறும் நிறம் கண்டு விருந்தோம்பி அரவணைத்தோம்
மேற்கு ஓர் திசை என்பதை மறந்து மேலைநாட்டவரிடத்தில்
மேன்மை நாம் தேடினோம் அடிமைகள் ஆனோம்.

மொழியால் வாழ்வியலால் மாநிலமாய் பிரிந்தால் என்ன
வேற்றுமைகள் தொலைத்து ஒன்றுபடுவோம் ஓர் கொடியின் கீழ்
தேசம் பெரியது அடையாளங்கள் உயிர் போன்றது
இரண்டும் ஓங்கும் ஓர் சமத்துவம் காண்போம்.

செல்வி

## Yaar mudhal song

We seek to establish the antiquity of our ancestors by looking for evidence in the corpses. Such people are the ones who are backward in evolution. If we seek the date of our Vedic literature, it predates your culture's start date. Imagine how much before we would have begun as a civilization... These people boast about crossing oceans to find our land. How in the first place did they know of its greatness? We thought since they come from the '*melai naadu*' (term for west, the word means upper lands literally) they are superior, and we expected them to behave better and ended up being their slaves. That is the translation of that song. Selvy thought the words were strong, yet maturely balanced.

Selvy had done the ice breaker. She slowly asked him, "hey, I know I was here in Chennai, but I couldn't join the *jallikattu* protests or even know about it. I was in class 11/12, remember?"

Her dad had given her the 'How to make friends' by Dale Carnegie. And she saw how this crucial rule always worked. No one wants to listen to you. So let them speak if you need friends.

Sendhan needed just that. He said, "*Akka, Jallikattu* is an animal stock selection process. The villagers have a maximum of 3-5 bulls in a village which would become sperm donors for the cows, by natural mating. The *jallikattu* festival is when the bulls are selected. The participants who volunteer to hug the bull's hump. *Eru thazhuvuthal* is another name for *jallikattu* which means hugging the bull. If the bull was able to run 200 metres with one or sometimes more than one human hanging on its hump or the *thimilu*, the bull wins. If not, the human wins the *salli* (coins) that is tied to the bull's horns, therefore *Jallikattu*.

The cows that win become the '*Kovil kalai*' or the 'Alpha male' for the village since these would be more virile. The ones that are weak would be castrated, their testicles crushed and only then they would pull bullock carts or plough fields.

The political issue about it was that western vested interests in selling semen of their breeds wouldn't be possible if they let the natural selection process continue. Their breeds are not adapted to the dry humid weather of our land and require a different fodder, which should again be bought from them. Our breeds are drought resistant and feed on the local leaves and the agricultural waste, like dried paddy plants or *vaikol* or the sediment left after the oil is extracted from coconuts and groundnuts. This is called *punnakku*. They are also fed, bran, called *thavudu*.

The Indian breeds would eventually be wiped out if the foreign semen was introduced, since the farmers would be forced to sell their cows to slaughterhouses. Since Tamilnadu consumes very little beef, most of it is exported. Indirectly those people are the ones that do these conspiracies."

Selvy asked why Sendhan hated the west so much. He said, "*Akka*, it is not hatred, it is disappointment with ourselves, that seems like anger. Take a country of your choice, take, for example, France, tell me how big that country is. May be the size of a district in Tamilnadu. Their tourist attractions are those that every district in India has. But look at how much they boast about it. Look at their pride with one Eiffel tower.

We have such marvellous pieces in every city. We have too much and that's why we don't realise the importance of things '*namakku arumai theryalai*'."

The invaders came in; we surrendered. Take the Jallianwala bagh massacre. There was this General Dyer who passed the shooting order, but who shot? Indian soldiers, who were part of the British Army. Imagine 10 soldiers were part of this. If they turned their guns towards Dyer, it would have been so easy. This hurts me, *akka*. I want to look at every possible way we can bring back the glory of our land.

I feel the same way about Africa. They are richly blessed. It is like this, *ka*. I have kidneys. Why would I sell it for someone to use it as a soccer ball?

One more thing *ka*, I don't know why diamond and gold are mined? Why do people use helium balloons at parties? Helium is mined. In fact, why don't we have any proof of mining activity in our archaeological discoveries, when we seem to have used iron for so long?

Why is it that chemistry only considers 'Uses 'and not 'Roles'?

There must be a reason some element is in some place, right? Wearing something mined by slaves just because it is a mark of status!!!"

Selvy felt so proud of Sendhan. It was a nice bonding session. Extremely awakening too. Sendhan was in class 10, but his knowledge and concern about the society made her feel belittled in front of him.

She was like the '*Kadivalam pota kudhirai*', a horse with eye blinders', running with sight only in one direction. It was his Deepavali break. Selvy taught him her periodic table song, which she made with the 'Closer' song as a parody. And they laughed and spent the whole day together, without watching TV or their mobile phones.

CHAPTER TWENTY

# Nathaniel

Dweepa's friend Branka had called Selvy to join her at a shooting club. Her husband was a member, and he worked in the research division of the Army in Switzerland. He had accompanied them as well.

Dweepa couldn't join, since Aakash was unmanageable now. She wanted to catch some sleep during the weekend.

Selvy wasn't sure if Branka would be another Lenka. She was hesitant. She seemed like a pleasant company. So, Selvy went.

The club seemed like a research lab, not an entertainment zone. She was expecting something like a bowling zone at a mall. Because she thought a country like switserland would have something far more fancy than her Anna University Alumni club. the only one she was a member of. However she had never used any of their facilities. She had never had such hobbies. Her hobby was listening to music.

They were received by an enthusiastic man, who seemed single, Selvy sensed his attempts to impress her.

He flaunted his aiming skills. After some awkward moments of silence, he asked Selvy,

"would you like to try?"

" I have never done this before!" she said.

" Let me help you" he said and put his arms around her like in a hug. Though he held her, she could feel that the touch wasn't uncomfortable, or with any malicious intent. It was with as much dignity as she liked. His perfume made her feel extremely drawn to him. She herself felt she was noticing many nice things about this man. some of these feelings are things Selvy never experienced till then. She felt it was alright to enjoy some flirtation without getting too serious about it.

Branka and her husband also seemed to have come there to spend some quality time together.

They then went to the cafeteria. Branka seemed very jovial, and Selvy never felt like she was talking to someone from another culture. She even shared how she felt like a tribal woman, who would be happy with just the sling bag carrying her son Aadiv, till the time he joined school.

Selvy also realised her life had been nomadic while she grew up. When Branka shared about their struggles as they moved to each place, she could relate to them. Selvy thought Branka would make a good Stand-up comedian. She was explaining the different dialects in each place she went to and how she used to mix everything and make new words.

Selvy recalled how she was accused of the same thing...

Her *Paati* used to imitate Selvy saying, "Selvy your friend said '*ki*' let's play" and asked her why she added Key to every sentence.

Selvy saw that the 'impressor-with-that-wonderful-deo' hadn't joined them immediately. He came back with some plates with marks of the bullet. The bullet holes were circled, and something was written on each.

He then joined them, and Selvy didn't know how time flew. Branka's husband shared about how expensive chemicals were. He was sharing about some of the new alloys and about why the work of research scientists like Selvy was crucial for so many applications.

He was sharing about the alloy that his lab had developed, which could make satellites lighter. He also shared that the metal plates were different pure elements and alloys which were being tried out for bullet proof material development.

Selvy felt extremely important, almost like a celebrity. She went back to her room with the lingering perfume of 'Nathaniel'.

She finally mustered courage and found his name before they came back. She was thinking of the perfect name they had chosen for him. '*Natham*' means smell.

She played back the conversation with Branka's husband, and it was her next clue. She took her notepad and scribbled. As they were preparing to leave, Nathaniel introduced his boyfriend to the group. She realised that he way Gay and was ashamed of how she had misunderstood his genuine care for flirtation. She sheepishly took leave and went home smiling to herself about the whole day's experiences.

CHAPTER TWENTY-ONE

# Turtle Walk

Sendhan's '*Ayutha ezhuthu*' gang was meeting for Turtle walk. An initiative that Selvy had been part of when she was in Chennai. Selvy and Yegna also volunteered to join. The volunteers had begun this initiative to conserve olive ridley turtles that came to nest and lay their eggs along the coastline. The volunteers met late at night, around 11:00 PM and walked a distance of 14km along the coastline in chennai and upon spotting a turlte trail, dug out the nested eggs and re-nested them in secure hatcheries. This was in an attempt to prevent the eggs from being preyed by stray dogs, and humans and other animals, which had been a regular affair. The hatchlings were sensitive to light and the developmental activities along the coastline, like the newly laid highway, were lit by streetlights all night. this caused the hatchlings to get disoriented and many moved to the road instead of to the shore. This had caused the species to become endangered for extinction. This happens between the months of February and April and after the nightlong walk, they check the hatchery for hatchlings ready to be released into the sea.

Orissa Balu sir, an authority in Turtle trails and Tamil explorers research, had come there that day and Sendhan was excited to meet him to seek his blessing. Selvy was meeting him for the first time. He was a material scientist, Selvy was very impressed that he was such an active person and that he had been pursuing his passion after retirement.

There were some newbies, and Sendhan enthusiastically began explaining that Turtles consider Tamilnadu their maternal home. They come home to lay their eggs. They trust us, '*machan*'. A slang word he pronounced with such a heavy Hindi accent, his friends asked him if he was a '*Sait*'. She could see how people like her must handle globalization with a pinch of salt.

"Hey this seems like that animated kid's movie Moana *da*." said the new boy.

Then Sendhan said, "the '*Thiraimeelar, thenpulathar*' the travellers of the south are linked to people in Tahiti and the Mayans too. The Mayan pyramid has the same Navagraha concept. These tribes shown in that movie are probably travellers like Tamils, or Tamils themselves.

The turtles could find directions and spot land. So, the seafarers of the Tamils used them in their ships. If there was a storm and they lost track of the direction, turtles could take them to the nearest land. There are communities in the South who wear thali (the holy thread or chain that is a mark of a wedding ceremony) with a turtle symbol on it."

In fact, even the temples, if they were ancient, would have the turtle holding the Flag mast. The turtle would point eastwards. So, when you go to the temple, you can see the position of the turtle and know which direction the temple was facing.

Selvy was getting goosebumps at the fact that her baby brother has collected such a lot of information at 15 years of age and was amazed at his enthusiasm towards his cultural roots and his natural urge to save its glory. She had a strong feeling that he was more suitable for the task that *chiththi* believed Selvy could do.

CHAPTER TWENTY-TWO

# Velum Mayilum

Selvy had already been convinced about the terrific potential of the seemingly harmless text Thirukkural. She was recalling her chitti mentioning something about an atom and the thirukkural. she quickly browsed to see what it was and was amazed.

"anuvai thulaiththu ezh kadal puguththi kuruga thariththa kural"- If you drilled an atom and filled it with the seven seas, that's how potent the shrunken Kural couplets are.

If the poem did not have the potential to be a scientific coded text, why couldnt she have found any other metaphor? And if Avvaiyaar knew the existence of atom. something modern science credits to John Dalton, it was something that only convinced Selvy that she was blessed to have been chosen to pursue this correlation.

She booked her tickets for going back to Aralvaimozhi with her findings so far. She was just 18 away from completing the *Arathuppal* chapter. If she did that, it would help her discover something *Chiththi* and Jeyaraman trusted her with. Infact, she also felt Bala paati was waiting for Selvy to get the breakthrough. She understood why she was chosen for this journey. No one else could establish some of the connections that she did as a Particle physicist.

She touched her forehead to see if there was some burning scar. Am I really the chosen one? And felt silly. What she was going to reveal wasn't fantasy. It is the greatest mystery of the time. A mystery that we need to bring out as Tamils. she knew that as a particle physicist she could correlate these logically as well. sometimes coincidences are crazy. like they say reality is stranger than fiction.

She was also amazed at the coding expertise of Valluvar. What a man! was he human, or was he some angel who had powers? was he sent down to the earth to guide us through a path of wisdom? And Avvaiyaar, what a woman!

She was convinced that we weren't carving out stones not to just display artistic or technological superiority, as a civilization. They seem to have dropped clues on stone, on palmleaf manuscripts on the texts and all ways possible for us to atleast reach the level they were at. It was the reason for the coding that she needed to crack. There can't be more substantial evidence.

She recalled their neighbour Annapoorni mami's house and there she had the answers for both adhigaram 23 and 24. She was eagerly waiting for that interaction.

CHAPTER TWENTY-THREE

# Annapoorni Mami's house

Rajam *paati*'s neighbour had invited *paati* for a function at their home.

"It is a *Sumangali Prarthanai*," she said.

*Paati* and *Mami* were besties from school. *Mami* also invited Selvy, saying, '*vethala paaku vangikka va ma*'. Come home to collect betel leaves and betel nuts. It is considered auspicious to give this to guests, according to Tamils.

The next morning, *Paati* told Selvy to stay at home till 1 PM and come there after lunch. *Paati* said that that was a ritual when the whole house waited for the women to eat first before the others. They did that along with some other event that had happened in their homes. Since a wedding was over, to honour the ancestral goddesses and seek their blessings for the new bride, they did the function.

*Mami*'s son had brought home a bride, Nandhini *akka*. Her daughter Gayathri *akka* was there too. Gayathri *akka* and Nandhini *akka* were besties. Selvy knew them from her days in Chennai. They were both trained in vocal Classical Carnatic music. They did concerts together. Parameswaran anna had married his sister's best friend. Parameswaran *anna* would be moving to Australia next month, said Gayathri. Selvy was excited to see them in traditional 9 yards (madisar) saree and felt why they had such a difficult costume.

*Mami* invited Selvy excitedly. The house was filled with guests. Parameswaran *anna*'s cousin Mythili was there too. Her son, Vaibav, was one year old, and they had his head shaved. Mythili *akka* said they had come back straight from Palani.

Everything in *mami*'s house triggered a hundred questions in Selvy's mind. Rajam *paati* sensed it and she called Annapoorni *mami* and said, "*ivalukku naraya kelvi kekanum. Ungalukku time irukkuma?* She seems to be curious about too many things, can you answer? Do you have time?"

Annapoorni *mami* was enthusiastic. She said, "it is good that you wish to ask. That is how one should be. If the procedure seems to convince you, follow it. There are many such things that i always wish children should be curious about. Instead of completely ignoring our cultural practices, curiosity might help you analyse their importance."

Selvy asked her what her profession was. Annapoorni *mami* said that she had studied Saiva siddhantham in University of Madras and she did '*Aanmeega sorpozhivu*' meaning she was a public speaker.

Selvy was happy that she got to meet someone of her Paati's age, who was not just a senior citizen, reading forwarded messages on social media, and was someone who had been formally educated in the field that she was talking about. Selvy always took pride in people who strived to be academically qualified, since that showed how committed they were to their passion. She felt happy to meet her in person and clarify many things.

Selvy then asked her about the poojai that day. *Mami* said that it was a form of ancestral worship. "We worship the elders who passed away, especially women. So the women who have lived in this family and passed away are worshipped and honoured. Everytime a girl is brought into this family through a wedding or a girl leaves this family by marrying off, is received of sent off after seeking the blessings of the ancestors of the family. You might notice that this ritual doesnt include any idol wordhip. It has the pictures of the ancestors of this family, and the offerings, if you notice are things women use to decorate themselves with. There is a mirror which reflects that each carries the soul which is the essence of the divine, within themselves. Another speciality of this event is that women of the house are expected to eat before the others can. The women who are invited to eat, are considered as representatives of our ancestors. After offering them food, they are also given gifts containing simple things that they might use to decorate themselves with, along with betel leaves, and nuts, turmeric, vermillon etc. " said Annapoorani *mami.*

Selvy asked her what she thought about languages, and about the never ending fight about which was more ancient.

Annapoorani *mami* shared," Languages are majorly impacted by the weather. Trying to speak Tamil in a cold country would be a challenge. In cold weather, one would find that their nostrils are blocked and sounds that required one to close their mouth fully would be difficult to pronounce as well. So those places would have different phonetic sounds. In tamil the alphabets have been seggregaed to three groups, based on how hard they sound. The first group *vallinam* has some of the hard sonding alphabets. The middle one *idaiyinam* has the gentler ones and the last group *mellinam* has all the soft sounds. When I grew up in tirunelveli, my teacher taught us tongue twisters. I recall two. One was to perfect the pronunciation of *vallinam* alphabets, the other was for idaiyinam. They are,

*'vikrama singapuraththu madaththu mudukku idukku iruttilirukkum karaththa karadiyai kollaathey'*

*and the other one is'*

*'thovaazhai kottaiyile kizhavan uzhudha puzhudhiyile, moovaazhaakku uzhakku nellukku ezhu vaazhaippazham'.*

Selvy tried saying them. Gayathri *akka* and Nandhini *akka* had joined her too and they had a hearty laugh...

*Mami* then shared whatever her spiritual guru had shared with her. "if you wished to explore which language was the first one that humans spoke, that would be tough to find out. But Tamil and sanskrit have been spoken during the same timeline. sanskrit has for unknown reasons, has discontinued to exist as a spoken language. But tamil is still spoken, retaining many of the words that existed way back thousands of years. Nature decides what to keep and what to drop. The very fact that nature chose tamil to be continued for these many years definitely shows its strength in some way. To me both are equal. She said she learnt both."

Nadhini and Gaythri went away as someone had called them. *Mami* did one funny thing, she hit a mosquito that sat on her and put it in a spider's web and said, "*konnal paavam, thinnal pochu*' meaning, it is a sin to kill, but it is rectified by feeding."

Gayathri rushed back and said, "Selvy be very careful with my mom. She is a public speaker and some topics can get her speaking for hours at a stretch, she said with a playful giggle.

Rajam *Paati* said, "No no dear, she has come prepared with a list of questions. Let her ask and get to know." Gayathri ran away as soon as she had come.

Selvy hesitantly asked her next question. "*Mami,* what do you think about non vegetarian food?"

Annapoorani *mami*, without cringing at the question, which felt inappropriately timed, shared, "we do not consume non vegearian food, since we believe that animal derived products might have an influence on our brain. They take a lot of time to digest and therefore the stomach's other activities remain largely unexplored, when one consumes meat. The hormones of animals are similar to those of humans and therefore, they do impact us. Our thoughts, emotions, such as anger, greed, stubbornness, fighting spirit, etc seem to be influenced by meat consumption. in fact you should ask your thatha about this too. As a Siddha doctor, he would tell you the kind of food that is suggested while taking siddha treatment. one that is bland and it is believed to be more healing.

In a way, people of tamilnadu are always considerate about life around and irrespective of how much they love non vegetarian food, you might observe that they refrain from consuming it during the breeding season of animals. even fishermen don't go out for fishing during the fish breeding seasons. Even if they catch small fish, they always set them free for them to grow to adulthood. our people are cultured. they are not barbaric. During the breeding season, which falls on the month of *purattaasi*, around September, you might see that there is Navaratri celebrations, when people cook lentils, sundal. This is to ensure that the protein requirements are met with plant proteins. "

Mythili *akka*'s baby Vaibav began taking his first steps. Everyone around began cheering him and Selvy, mami and Paati joined the cheering squad too. Vaibav got excited and sat giggling with his baby squabbles. However, he didnt disappoint his audience. He slowly stood up holding onto the nearby furniture and began his ramp walk again with renewed enthusiasm.

Selvy decided to head home. As she sensed that mami had loads of chores. She had a lot of information to ruminate anyways.

CHAPTER TWENTY-FOUR

# Deficiency and Overdose

Ida had been to a conference about water quality analysis, in Sweden. The conference had participants from about 40 countries, and some were discussing the problems they faced with the desalination process. Her role in CERN was unique. As a sincere and hard-working person, Ida was one of the most loved persons in the lab.

Selvy had successfully cracked 24 *Adhigarams* now and 25 and above seemed to get more and more tricky. Though she was listening to Ida's experiences at the conference, her heart was looking for some clue from somewhere to crack why Thiruvalluvar had a chapter about vegetarianism.

Ida was mentioning about Salts of a desalination plant and how some countries like India have always used sea salt by drying it on beds and how countries insist on Iodine fortification. She mentioned that making some things compulsory wasn't necessary at all.

Selvy asked her why she felt so, and Ida explained that Iodine deficiency causes Thyroid issues. So, if people had the issue, they could consume iodised salt. But if there was no issue with their hormones, adding Iodine compulsorily, would have more than necessary in their blood, right?

Selvy at once got the connection with *Adhigaram* 25. So that rule was geographical location specific. She was waiting for Ida to finish her enthusiastic sharing process and then noted down her thoughts in the Notepad. She was amazed at how even a chapter she never thought made sense was now relevant.

Selvy was browsing between Karka Kasadara, Youtube channel where Ilangai Jeyaraj *ayya* was explaining and the other videos from America and Nottingham University, the exploratorium etc.

She found the next connection within minutes. It was getting crazy that a chapter such as penance would connect this well with science and that there was finer decoding and a lot of concentration required from her end.

She felt that this was exactly how anyone who is a seeker of any truth that mattered to them would feel. the state of penance. She felt like she herself was in a penance. She touched her head, trying to check if there was a matted knot, that had come there as well, and laughed at her own plight.

But as she was about to complete *Arathuppal*, her conviction towards the text increased by leaps and bounds. It felt as if she had taken up an important role as someone who would have to bring back the lost glory. If one text is this vast and advanced, what about the others. She took out the list she felt like exploring next. And was telling herself that it would be one after another. She also worried if there would be someone to help her understand the others. That Tamil was not something she was confident about pursuing on her own.

*Adigaram* 27 was another hard one to crack. She felt she needed to discuss with her Shah uncle regarding this.

CHAPTER TWENTY-FIVE

# Movies, Fun, Chat....

Selvy, Sendhan and Yegna went out for a movie with Sendhan's new friend Mohammed Raahil and his mom Badur Nisha. The movie was a time loop based one and Selvy was intrigued by the kinds of concepts they chose for movies in Tamil. She had seen movies about various aspects of the society and was already beginning to appreciate every aspect of Tamil.

Selvy's mom was a Rahmaniac and she would even recall a movie scene's background score from a movie for which the Oscar winner, A.R.Rahman had scored music. In fact, Selvy was forced to learn to play the Keyboard as a tribute to this generation's music genius.

Nisha was also a huge movie buff; the car had the FM radio playing on all the way. They went to a theme park and the theatre near it.

Whatever Selvy did, her head was spinning around all that she recently got to know. She needed concrete evidence however, to prove that since her scientific analysis was always urging her for it.

Nisha was unique. She was not the muslim Selvy had imagined. Selvy had no muslim friends before that. During her schooling at Gwalior, she had hardly seen muslims being this interactive and lively. Nisha was independent and a fun person. She shared that her mom had returned from Haj and that their family was very religious. Yet she seemed free-spirited. The topic went from that to Dr.Abdul Kalam and his greatness and how his death was mourned by every household as if one of their own grandparents passed away, to every possible topic. He was one person who had transcended the boundaries of religion and had been like an elderly person in every Indian family.

She then shared, her dad had been a huge fam of the actor turned politician of yester years, M.G.R. She shared that her father's ancestors were from Srilanka and they moved to a village named Thondi. Because of which they had a huge adulation for MGR. He used to sing songs from MGR movies and that he would remember each line and each lyric. She shared that those songs were very socially stimulating. She mentioned songs such as '*En endra keLvi*' which was about the stimulation of society to ask the question 'Why' and not blindly follow some practice. She mentioned another song '*chinna payale.*' which urged children to be fearless and cautious about people who could be cunning.

The topic then went to *Kalaignar* Karunanidhi, another leader who made the 'Valluvar Kottam'. Selvy made a mental list in her head for a place to visit next time. They also spoke about various things that have become the trend after the Jallikattu protest, about Hip Hop Tamizha, and Tamil rap and the Tamizhi script sensitization through a song. From there again the topic went to Keezhadi archaeological site.

Selvy got reminded again about Jeyaraman and the Thirukkural.

Nisha shared that movies in English, such as Matrix and Interstellar were so tough to understand. Selvy explained them. She also shared that Doctor Strange was another interesting movie. Selvy's choice was Japanese Anime. She felt some of them had so many similarities with concepts in India.

Selvy and Nisha also discussed books that have become movies, some have been better than the books and some have had the core of the book missing. They discussed Hollywood movies which were based on books, such as the Harry Potter series and the movies based on books written by Dan Brown. Nisha shared about a mysterious book 'Ponniyin Selvan', filming which always caused some bad omen. They also discussed about all the movies that were based on kings of the land. She shared about the temples that were built during the period of Raja Raja Cholan.

Selvy was excited, and they discussed the Harry Potter series. Nisha shared that one of her neighbours, who was a staunch Hindu shared that Harry Potter wouldn't have had the scar, had he applied *kumkumam* (vermilon) and *Vibhuthi* (Holy ash) on his forehead.

Selvy found one more question in her mind triggered with that. They then started chatting again and were sharing how the book became a rage and how their teachers were sometimes Umbridge, sometimes Professor McGonagal etc.

CHAPTER TWENTY-SIX

# The 'Pottu'

Geneva, Switzerland

Selvy had by now got so involved in the decoding process that she spent more time with her notepads, searching all over the internet since it had now taken her over completely. She began understanding their advancements and how scientific quest of the Tamils and how they never harmed the environment in any way. *Adhigaram* 28 was easier to crack. But *adhigaram* 27 made Selvy wonder if this much could be possible in the past!

Suddenly, she recalled some of the incidents that happened in Chennai. *Paati*'s neighbour had mentioned things that Selvy thought would be significant. She couldn't wait now, she texted *athai*'s number.

She typed, 'Hi Renu, need some information for my work, Urgent!'

Renuka was online and she responded more quickly than Selvy expected.

Selvy asked, as if her intuition suggested so. "Renu, why do Tamils use *Kumkumam* on the forehead? Does that have some scientific reason too?

Renuka was excited to answer. Having been brought up in Mylapore, the culturally rich part of Chennai, she had been searching for stuff like his to restore the glory of India. Renuka was a gynaecologist, so she explained in terms that Selvy understood instantly.

She asked, "why do you think plants are green?"

Selvy said, "because they have chlorophyll"

Renuka explained, "an object appears in that colour which is reflected by it. If you see a red coloured apple, it means, apple reflects red colour. In other words, the objects absorb other colours, apart from that which is reflected."

"In the Visible spectrum, which has the longest wavelength?", asked Renuka.

Selvy typed "Red."

"What is beyond red?" asked Renuka.

Selvy said, "Microwaves, radio waves, gamma radiations etc."

Renuka then began typing a long response. "The red of the *kumkumam* that is made by Tamils is not a dye that is used in other parts of the country. It is made by mixing turmeric with an alkali. You might recall that turmeric is acidic. It is also a natural pH indicator. The compounds in Turmeric are capable of absorbing long wavelength radiations, beyond Red. Tamils also apply turmeric over their skin. This is also for diagnostic purposes. The pH of the skin is slightly acidic. Turmeric stays yellow in acidic pH and turns maroon in alkaline pH. Cancer cells have a more acidic pH (around 6.5) than normal cells. Even though they thrive in acidic environments. Alkalinity would kill cancer cells since the pH difference would become drastic.

You might recall that radio waves, microwaves and gamma radiations are identical to the brain waves in their frequency and can influence them. Thus, keeping the *kumkumam* would help people in staying protected from every type of damage to their brain."

Selvy wondered, "so there was this radiation safety practice incorporated into the culture! Without letting them know why this was suggested. The temples were the treatment centres, according to whatever Selvy's grandmother explained. It helped in bringing this damage control protocol into a cultural practice. Brilliant!" Selvy thought. She had now cracked 27- *kooda ozhukkam*, bad habits.

Selvy asked about vegetarianism. Renu said, meat consumption adds to the muscle mass. However it doesnt contribut much to bone strength or bone density. Bone density requires minerals such as Calcium, Manganese, etc. which are not found in meat at all.

She thought the next two chapters were easy to interpret. She browsed the list of meteorites that have fallen on Earth so far and made some notes with the information.

For the next one, all that was required was recalling whatever she studied in Class 11 and 12. As she browsed, it was interesting to note the colour of the Statue of Liberty and the connection this had with spiders etc.

She was getting closer to the completion of Arathuppal and she was waiting to head back home to share her findings with Valli *chiththi*.

CHAPTER TWENTY-SEVEN

# Pazhani-Navapashanam

Chennai.

Gayathri *akka*'s cousin's baby was at home when Selvy came back from the movie. *Thatha* and *Paati* were playing with him. He had begun talking slowly and *Paati* was trying to speak to him in the baby babble. It was funny for Selvy to see a 70-year-old and a 1-year-old playing together.

After they went home, Selvy asked *Paati*, why do they shave off a baby's hair?

*Paati* said, "*thatha* has a lot of theories about it. He has his own research about *Navapashanam* too."

She knew *Thatha* was a Siddha doctor. But never asked him about his job. Before she could begin speaking, *Thatha* understood and started explaining about Siddhars and their method for healing.

*Thatha* said, "They believe that Lord Murugan would save the child. It is common practice for *Tamils* to tonsure their head after the child is one year old. The hair is given as an offering. The temple at Pazhani is unique. The statue there is made of something called the *Navapashanam*. These are 9 types of poisons which are supposed to have healing properties. There is a popular verse you might have heard, ' the effect of a substance is in its dosage'. There was a popular saying that 'too much of anything is poisonous', even if that was food. The siddhars read the same sentence as a coded information. they wondered if the dosage of a poison was diluted would that have medicinal properties. This was attempted and very successfully executed by them. You might now see that various medicines, such as blood clotting factors, are actually derived from snake venom. If you visit the temple, you might notice that the statue is slowly wearing off and they have off-late stopped the abhishekam. Which means, pouring various things and water over the statue and distributing it as a prasadam.

Siddha medicine has a lot of information about herbs and their medicinal benefits.

Selvy asked, what was the difference between Ayurveda and Siddha. Thatha said that Ayurveda and Siddha were very similar. Both are based on using nature to reset the body's functions. Both are based on how the three doshas, vatha, pitha and kapha impact the body and how their imbalance is the core of any disease. These three doshas are nothing but the energies that drive the functioning of the body. Siddha medicine uses herbs ssourced based on the work of siddhars, processed and administered as concoctions or tonics orally. Ayurveda uses oil based preparations and the treatment includes massages which have now become very popular with people.

Thatha noticed the conversation getting extremely academic and serious. everyone was watching him with rapt attention. He said, "I have a friend who learnt all three, do you know what his name board reads? Dr.Suresh, USA. That is for Unani, Siddha, and Ayurveda."

Selvy burst out laughing. She said, "so people think he has learnt that from the US?"

Thatha laughed and said, "yes."

Paati called everyone to continue the conversation at the dinner table. As everyone took seats, Thatha began explaining that Ayurveda was derived from Sushrutha, a Sanskrit medical scientist's work and Siddha considered *Agathiyar* as its *guru*.

"Siddha medicine used rare herbs and concoctions from mountains and the treatments involve fasting and diet alterations. Ayurveda targets the muscles and nerves, and they have massages with medicated oils. Nowadays, these have penetrated each other so much that even I can call myself USA," he said, and winked.

*Thatha* mentioned that Siddha believed that the effect of a medicine was in the dose. And that small quantities of poison have medicinal properties. They even consider too much of anything is harmful, even water beyond the amount required is dangerous.

Selvy realised that it was true.

*Thatha* explained that Siddha medicines were stronger and so the patients had to follow the prescribed diet more strictly.

Ayurveda has been marketed more efficiently by the government of Kerala and their department of tourism. So, people don't know that there is an ancient medical science called siddha here.

He also shared that, even today there are some siddhars in places like Thiruvannamalai, Podhigai, Nilgiris, Kolli hills etc. Even today many people consider their treatment most effective and avoid going to hospitals.

One of the practices of Tamils has been tonsuring of the head after one year of birth of a child.

Thatha also shared how his grandfather used to do things like *Pal kavadi*, which was a ritual. The *kavadi* is decorated with Peacock feathers, he added. They also chant *Velum, Mayilum thunai.* Some people even pierce the *Vel*, a pointy poky metallic needle through their skin, mouth etc.

Thatha began singing, "*oru pozhudhu iru charana nesathevai ariyene...*" he said that was his favourite *Thiruppugazh*. That's another book full of songs that are sung in praise of Murugan.

Selvy asked how many texts there are in Tamil. She also asked which was the oldest. Paati then explained that there are many, that the oldest is Tholkappiyam. And she gave her extensive list of literature. Selvy was already overloaded with information and food from the movie, and she dozed off as Rajam spoke.

CHAPTER TWENTY-EIGHT

# Biosafety guidelines

One of the routine conferences in any lab is about Biosafety guidelines and modifications in practices in the lab. These are conferences that many hate to attend. Since they feel that the case studies presented are exaggerated.

The series of lectures this time was done most efficiently according to Selvy. Ever since her Thirukkural Project began, she has been an extremely keen observer. She felt that her doubts about the Tamil society being most advanced could find some way to prove from any and every extra information.

The speaker began by saying, "As scientists, we feel that understanding anything is by breaking things apart. We are curious as toddlers, and if you recall what toddlers would do after they dismantle a toy, we are capable of leaving things as such since our brains are programmed in such a way that we care little about other things and consider our projects to be of utmost importance.

The dismantled parts of the toy might poke the parent, the nanny or another child or the child that broke the toy itself. Similarly, our experiments and their dangers are to be considered with as much care as we do our experiments."

With that strong an introduction, the speaker spoke about some of the elements which have caused quite a lot of damage in the past, with respect to radiations,

The next speaker was presenting about the overdose of some chemicals.

Selvy sat there picturing herself as the Pillaiyar, with elephant ears as the receivers and as if the intention from her imaginary pot belly urged the speaker to touch upon the exact thing that Selvy had been looking for. The speaker mentioned that Zinc was an element that was part of several syrups and was believed to boost immunity. However, overdose of Zinc would spike the testosterone levels and would cause hormonal imbalance that results in fertility issues in both men and women. There were things that she had cracked and was shocked to see some *Kurals* translating to whatever the presenter explained.

She now knew the answers for *adhigaram* 30 and 31.

Next up was another crazy connection about linking a semiconductor with killing. She got answers for it while one presenter spoke about some of the banned compositions.

She realised that whatever was being discussed were technically issues of the present day and age. It blew her mind to think that she was able to draw parallels to something compiled thousands of years ago. she felt proud of being a drop connected to the immortal stream that culturally irrigated her great land.

CHAPTER TWENTY-NINE

# Carnatic music and 432 Hz

Gayathri *akka* and Nandhini *akka* had been practising for their concert together and Selvy heard the music and went to their house to listen. She had never seen people sing carnatic music live. She was fascinated by their dedicated practice. They had an electronic shruti box. With just an electronic drone as the accompanying instrument, they were able to transport the listener to ancient times with their rendition. The drone tuner might be modern but the songs they practised were from the Bhakthi period, centuries ago. It was a divine experience.

Selvi had learnt to play the keyboard and was aware of the notes in Western classical music. She knew some Music theory as well and knew how notes are organised in the western scale. She wanted to know more about Carnatic music and about the same time, the two decided to take a short coffe break. The trio sat in the living room and then Selvi asked them how different the two were.

Nandhini's mom taught Music at the Music college, so Nandhini was quick to respond and began explaining enthusiastically. She said that Carnatic music was highly scientific. The scales in Western are analogous to the Ragas in Carnatic.

In western music, there were only scales that had all the notes being played. But in Carnatic music, there was scope for having lesser notes in some ragas. The ragas were organised by the Melakartha scheme, and this was the grouping based on what combination of musical notes were present in them, like a probability distribution. The ragas of the Melakartha scheme are considered mother ragas from which daughter ragas arise.

She said that the names of the ragas were chosen through the *Katapayadi* scheme. She recognised the word immediately through Jeyaraman's explanation for *Aathichudi* decoding.

Selvi wondered why tamils were culturally obsessed with going to the maximum limit of excellence in every area. even music which is considered one for entertainment, seems to be so technically profound that she wondered if this could have been an acquired habit or was etched in their DNA.

Selvy asked why the sound of the music sounded different from western, tonally! They said, the difference is in tuning. Gayathri said, the western system tuned their instruments to 440 Hz frequency and the Indian instruments are always tuned to 432Hz. She said 4+3+2 = 9 that's a Tesla number.

What! another Tesla reference, thought Selvy.

They asked her to try a song and Selvy made a small mistake and it went off note. And the two girls jerked. Gayathri then said, the notes seem to play on our nerves and an incorrect combination feels like we had a short circuit. She shared that the Tamil language has rightly named the strings of a musical instrument. They are called 'nerves-*narambu*'

Selvy was recalling the biology lessons about nerves and electrical transmission. She also recalled the static charge that we sometimes get when we wear a synthetic dress or go down a slide.

They mentioned that some ragas had healing properties and mentioned that there was a violin maestro who mentioned that Raga Bhairavi could heal the heart.

Selvy wondered about whatever her *Paati* told about temples and was imagining the devadasis in Nurse's costumes as diagnostic assistants. Once the diagnosis was done, they sang it out to the people in the the Temple kitchen who would then make specific concoctions for the person who had been given the prescription. The devotees informed the priest of their natal planetary positions and the star under whose influence they were born. Based on the current planetary positions and how favourable or otherwise the astrological implications were, they were given a *prasadam* with healing herbs infused in them. She imagined a small crowd of about 20 at once in the temple and this process happenening seamlessly. However she suddenly felt herself part of a crushing crowd of devotees, standing in a long queue. She openend her eyes startled.

She asked if these were only in Carnatic music. Then Gayathri added that the village women have songs called '*PaN*", which is considered to be the precursor that evolved into Carnatic music.

Selvy cursed herself for being so ignorant about the richness of her motherland. She wondered if any other culture would explain their practices and the reasons for them in this great detail. She was also imagining how the land would have been in the past.

She asked the girls how long they have been learning Carnatic music. They said they began singing at the age of 5. There was a mami who came home and it in fact takes about 12 years for someone to get on stage. Nandhini said, these days parents are so impatient and have begun appreciating even sub-standard talent. She shared that children have to learn to listen to 'No'. Appreciating each and every action would only take the whole community to mediocrity.

They also shared that the schools should also stop giving prizes for each kid. An athlete couldn't be identified if everyone was given a prize. In the intention to make sure children are not disappointed, we are also making room for truly talented children to lose interest in pushing their limits and performing.

They discussed politics, reservation policy and how it has helped many, the mid-day meal program for educating children at the same time feed them, the subsidised canteens, and the government run alcohol shops, which were a menace etc. They were discussing as if they were the next political strategisits.

It was deepavali the next day and Nandhini was packing her bags to go to her mom's place with *Anna*. It is the first deepavali after their wedding and it is customary to spend the first diwali, the *thalai* deepavali at the girl's mom's place.

Selvy bid them bye and was feeling she had over eaten the Deepavali snacks that Annapoorani mami had brought as they chatted. Annapoorani mami had also packed all the sweets and savouries to take home also. She was feeling so full that she felt along with the crackers, her stomach would explode too.

CHAPTER THIRTY

# Lunar Sage and realisation

Dweepa had asked Selvy to come home suddenly. Selvy went there hoping to find time to compile the notes. The lab had become a little hostile to her since and everybody complained about her becoming too preoccupied and she had been way behind her schedules in the lab. All that she was carrying out were routine detector recordings. She had not analysed them for the past one week. She was more enthusiastic about heading home with Arathuppal. She barely had 5 more *adhigarams*. She felt she would get the answers for all of them soon.

Dweepa had to help the neighbour, Yuktha, let out their home to students. Her neighbour was away in America for 3 years.

Dweepa mentioned that she had to supervise the painting of the house and was sharing about how smart her neighbour was. It was all about what would be more economical. She said her neighbour had houses in almost 5 countries and all were fetching rent. And this house had 3 bedrooms with a bath attached and if it had been Dweepa, she would have let it out to a single family. But the neighbour wanted to make the most of everything.

She shared that one of Gautham's relatives was exactly like her neighbours and that they would have a lot of property but wouldn't want to spend anything. They detested Dweepa, since she was like the person who would break their stable family. Dweepa never asked them for any money. But they had been telling Dweepa's in-laws that a person who isn't like them would break the values of their family and exhaust whatever they had.

Dweepa shared that they felt they were the chosen ones. Including a person who doesn't have the same ideology would mutate their gene pool.

Selvy recalled that her grandparents had the whole upper floor empty for their children to come and stay whenever they came. And that renting out would have made them quite rich. But her parents and grandparents didn't believe in having more than what was necessary. They didn't hoard.

They spent carefully and saved some. But had always taught her a different set of values.

She suddenly recalled the *adhigarams* that were pending. *Nilaiyamai*(instability), *Thuravu* (renunciation) and *Meiyunardhal* (Self-realisation) were now making sense. When we have the scope for making more money and yet choose to live a life of modesty, then we have reached the stage of renunciation, the mental maturity to let go...

She was Selena, the lunar sage. Someone who would only conduct when activated with light... the light of knowledge...

CHAPTER THIRTY-ONE

# Deepavali

It had been quite a few years since they had celebrated Deepavali as a family, Selvy thought. Since Selvy grew up in the North, Selvy felt Deepavali was an inevitable festival. She had then been influenced by all her classmates about pollution due to noise of crackers and had stopped bursting them. So, for over 7 years, she had not burst crackers at all. This year, since the government had allotted times of the day when people can burst crackers, there seemed some enthusiasm.

She wondered if Annaporani *mami* and Rajam *paati* would have reasons for Tamilian Deepavali celebrations too.

*Paati* woke everyone up at 4.30 AM and asked everyone to apply oil on their head. It was gingely oil heated and cooled, with few whole pepper pods inside. Selvy had lived in Chennai for 2+4 years. But she never felt like asking 'why' they had this custom for Deepavali.

She also noticed that they made oily snacks during Deepavali and there was also a ginger based '*legiyam*', a medicinal sweet, that was given as soon as they woke up. She was asked to eat that on an empty stomach. They then wore new clothes and went out to burst crackers.

Sendhan was quick to ask this time. The sudden interest to know everything about Tamil traditions had begun nudging both of their minds.

*Thatha*, the Sidhdha doctor, began explaining it this time. He said the Tamils had oriented everything they did to the circadian rhythm. They had the light and dark, like the yin and yang in every aspect of time. So, they had the day divided into time till Sunlight was available and time after sunset. A week began with Sunday and ended with Saturday. Days are influenced by celestial objects and each day was assigned the name based on which astronomical object could influence the most. Thus Sunday was controlled by the Sun. Monday by moon and Saturday was under the control of Saturn, the last planet that could influence earth. A month was divided into Krishna patcham (Krishna meant dark) and Shukla patcham.

So, this was the waxing and waning moon concept, confirmed Selvy.

The year was divided into months when the earth moved towards and away from light. Sendhan asked if it was the equinox and solstice. And thatha said, "yes".

Sendhan was in 10$^{th}$ grade and so could recall the 6$^{th}$ standard geography lesson. *Thatha* continued, "The festivals for Tamils begin with the Tamil New year which coincides with the time of the year when the Indian subcontinent was facing the sun and the time when it is closest to the sun in the elliptical orbit. That falls on," *thatha* paused, and sendhan replied, "April 14$^{th}$." *Thatha* resumed his wisdom sharing, "The summer months are extremely hot and humid so these months we do not have any festivals. It is after *Aadi masam*, which falls between July and August that the rains begin in Tamilnadu. That month is devoted to crop selection through a festival called '*Mulaippari*' festival , in the agricultural zones. Villagers usually keep a stock of whatever they produce. A portion of this is used and sprouts are made. The whole village prepares this sprout basket. The one that grew best is then used as seed stock of the village.

Women are involved in *Mulaipari* preparation for which they go through a stringent routine of fasting, and daily hygiene.This gives the men time to recover from the summer months which would lower the sperm counts."

There was more that *Thatha* shared. "The year then has the *pillaiyar chathurthi*, when we make clay models of the *pillaiyar*, add 21 different herbs of medicinal importance, and dispose of them in a nearby water body. The clay would line the water catchment areas since it is after chathurthi that rains begin in Tamil nadu. The festival of Deepavali is celebrated in various parts of the country for various reasons But in Tamilnadu, there are several things attached to one practice."

Selvy said to herself, "as expected."

*Thatha* said, "In Tamilnadu, Deepavali is celebrated when the monsoon is about to end. The last spurt of rain falls after the festival. The monsoon lasts for about 2-3 months. The soil would be eroded off its minerals. With the rains, there would be formation of mould and fungi all over.

Thus, the scientific Tamils came up with this brilliant way to tackle these. They made oil-based snacks so that people had their gut lined with oils. They applied oil all over the body. The crackers that are made in Sivakasi are indegenous and have a composition that would replenish the soil's NPK fertilisers. The gunpowder mix has Potassium nitrate, Carbon, and Sulphur along with Aluminium, which gives the sparkles. Coloured sparkles are because of Barium and Strontium. The amounts of which have been regulated by the government. The bursting of crackers would seed the clouds with fertiliser mix.

The Sulphur would react with the atmospheric moisture and pour down as acid rain. The natural pH of soil in Tamil nadu is alkaline and rice cultivation requires neutral pH. Thus, celebration of Deepavali in Tamil nadu has an environmental benefit and not harm.

The Sulphur from the crackers gets into our skin and since it is soluble only in oil, we have the tradition of the oily snacks and oil bath. The chemical element would heal people who could have been affected by fungal infections during the rains.

The Sulphur from our body is washed away with Shikakai, which coagulates the Sulphur, making it soluble in water and less harmful for the flora and fauna of the lakes, rivers, and the sea.

The sound of the crackers would help in providing that adrenaline rush that helps keep the heart pumping well, since the next few months are winter."

"what is the role of this hormone? asked thatha, looking at Sendhan.

"Fight or flight hormone- adrenaline." answered Sendhan, promptly.

Paati, Yegna and Selvy, who had all joined and had been sitting around listening intently, clapped for Sendhan.

"100 marks", said thaththa, and continued. When the body senses some danger, it produces adrenaline, which increases the heart rate and helps it pump more effectively. The body during deepavali, would already be dull trying to digest all the oily savouries and sweets. In order to get the body alert and ready to face the winter that would follow, this proves as a fun way to reset. In fact the blocks if any in the blood vessels would get cleared automatically. The crackers and their noise pollution related stories are baseless. Noise pollution by vehicles, air pollution through vehicles or factories is far more than the two to three days of crackers.

Selvy felt goose bumps at the level of thought that has gone into each and every event.

She didn't know how much of all this was intended. Didn't know if thatha was telling the truth or not. She did observe that Deepavali in her house was never a prayer to some specific god.

*Thatha* said, "he wasn't a religious person. But believed in Nature's power and had there been a choice, he would call his way of life Aseevagam, where it is about believing in a supreme power and was against using fire to offer food to the divine that would burn and char it."

Selvy asked *thatha* about non vegetarian food. *Thatha* said, "it has been region specific. Tamils have been capable of understanding all the life forms around them. They only consumed non vegetarian food on particular times of the year that the animals have bred. They have never wiped out any species."

In fact, he suggested that if agriculture was right, that is, mass production of food by preparing the land and letting land only produce one species of plant was right, then farming animals and consuming them can't be questioned. If they consume, they make sure they have stocks too.

He said, "we are vegetarians by choice. Our family doesn't consume non-vegetarian food and wouldn't even get tempted to eat meat, since it is a principle, not just practice in our family. At the same time we don't judge another for their preferences. we only need to be compassionate to every living being."

CHAPTER THIRTY-TWO

# Arathuppal

The last two *adhigarams* of *arathuppal* were remaining.

Selvy's boss was furious with her. She had rescheduled her presentation the previous month too. Her boss, Chaitanya said she was giving her one last chance to prove herself. She would otherwise have to terminate her fellowship.

Selvy felt very embarrassed. She came to CERN with such a big dream but now it was as if Thiruvalluvar, Valli *chiththi* and Bala *Paati* had possessed her.

She decided to pause the two *adhigarams* and concentrate on finishing her presentation. Her tickets were booked, and she didn't want to go to India without fixing her reputation at CERN.

As she sat down, it was as if Valluvar guided her with clues. She played the whole sequence of events in her head.

She got educated with a focussed dream of getting to her dream lab, CERN, and she did.

The Nataraja statue led her to speak to her *chiththi*.

*Chiththi* took her to Podhigai hills and showed her the ஃ. She also met Thuthukkudi Jeyaraman and learnt how the Thirukkural needed to be approached.

She learnt so much about how scientific the Tamils were and how rich the culture was.

After getting back, she cracked 5 adhigarams.

She slowly opened her tear filled eyes, and let those warm drops of nectar flow through her cheeks. She took the notepads and looked at how easily *Kadavul vazhthu* associated with ஃ.

The 6$^{th}$ was easy in many ways, but two kurals were quite tricky. The *koozh* and the *isai*. She then easily cracked till 10. Again 11 was demanding. Then 14, then 15, 16 and 17 and 18 were easier.

20 made her understand that valluvar wasn't a saint sitting and meditating to find out about these and got to know answers through his divine vision (*gyana drishti*).

He seems to have had hands-on experience,

she thought. 21, 22, 23, 24,25 were all tough to crack too.

Now she had to work on two more *adhigarams*.

Her boss' voice frightened her again.

she closed her eyes again. The GSI Helmholtz Centre for Heavy Ion Research (GSI Helmholtzzentrum für Schwerionenforschung) in Darmstadt, Germany, said an inner voice. The lab that was dedicated for making new elements. She recalled seeing a flyer about a student exchange program from CERN to this lab.

She then got an idea. She thought she would crack the Thirukkural further and get the code that Valli *chiththi* explained in her *Aathichudi* decoding process. Use that to write a presentation and make it like a research proposal without mentioning anything about the source of the idea.

She could present the idea to the scientific community, try it out and then get to that pedestal from where she would be heard. And then, tell the whole world about Tamil and Valluvar.

But was her decoding correct? Was Thirukkural having the potential to get her to that place. Will the lab, leave alone the scientific community, take her proposal seriously. Will they feel that she is capable? Will they say that she was a profound researcher, or a dellusional one? There were a million questions, tribulations storming her mind.

She had begun gauging her thoughts again... She couldn't decide which path was right. Proving the potential of Thirukkural in a Lab or through a work of literature, a book or by working with a Tamil research group! Her heart said Tamil and Thirukkural while her brain said Lab.

CHAPTER THIRTY-THREE

# Dakshin Chitra

Selvy has been in touch with her friends in Anna and Madras University and they have been in touch with her for help. Universities that are managed by the government charge nominal fees and therefore have funding issues and must spend wisely. So, priority for research labs is usually given to purchase of chemicals and glassware. Libraries have reference books that would be helpful for students who study Masters courses.

Research scholars would need to refer to scientific journals so that they are able to ensure that the research is at par with other labs. Sometimes specific procedures/protocols published in journals need to be refered to. But scientific Journals have a huge subscription fee. So, research scholars who go abroad for post-doctoral research or other opportunities, always help their contacts with things like these. So, it is common practice to stay in touch with anyone abroad.

Selvy has always been a humble kid and she was prompt with sending scientific articles for her friends here.

This time, it was a unique request from her friend at the Crystallography and Biophysics Department, University of Madras. They had grown crystals of a protein. Their senior was in France. Since the student here couldn't travel, because of lack of funds, the sample had to be passed on. In fact, the data collection was going to be at the beamline allotted for Crystallography, at CERN. So, she would just need to take the sample to CERN and safely keep it till it was collected.

Sendhan wanted to visit Dakshina Chitra, which had Heritage homes, and the Cholamandalam Artist's village. He also wanted to see the crocodile park and snake park, which were at such a distance that the trip could include the University campuses.

So, Selvy, Yegna and Sendhan, went to Dakshina chitra first. There were heritage homes from all parts of the country and all walks of life, each displaying details about their architechture, interiors etc. Sendhan and Selvy were particularly interested in the Tamil homes.

There were art galleries too. Selvy saw some contemporary art, abstract paintings in fact. She hadn't imagined a traditional looking Heritage home site would have contemporary paintings displayed. She felt thoroughly impressed with the art gallery.

They then proceeded to the Cholamandalam Artist village. There was a museum. She saw many exhibits, but among them there was a sealed chart of Tamil fonts. She thought it was interesting and took a picture of it..

There was a Pot making workshop, Sendhan and Selvy made some pots, they could also visit a weaver's house, an artist's house and could see them at work. It was an exceptional and enlightening experience. She saw the Kolams. In fact, she was making a mental note of all that she had missed out while growing up.

After having lunch on their way back, they went to the crocodile park. Sendhan had seen a video about the Crocodile Park maintenance, and he wanted to interact with the vets there.

Yegna casually said, "we are going to see dinosaurs." Selvy was surprised. Then Yegna said, "do you know that crocodiles had the capacity to even digest iron?

Look at the language and its beauty. The animal which has stayed since the era of dinosaurs, is named '*Mudalai*', meaning from early on... *Mudal* meant first." Sendhan was so excited, "*amma, #munnorgal muttalgal illai.* Ancestors were not fools," he said, and began typing it out with a picture of it collaged with a mosasaurus, its predecessor, and posted it on Insta, instantly.

Selvy then met Kanagasabai Anna from University. He had packed the crystals in tubes and sealed them in a flask filled with liquid Nitrogen. He also handed a letter of permission, since she was carrying a chemical sample. And it would need clearance from customs. Even though her dad was a customs officer, she wanted to make sure that she had the right papers.

CHAPTER THIRTY-FOUR

# The presentation and the decisions

Selvy was extremely thrilled with what she had prepared. She was going to leave two days after the presentation.

Her *chiththi* had sent a coded text message. She decided to look at it after the presentation, and she told herself... 'two more days, and I would be in Aralvaimozhi anyways'. Selvy was extremely tense. And the presentation was a chance to prove herself to her lab.

Selvy prayed to Valluvar silently, "*Ayya*, I know what you have done. If it is not me then who. I promise to you that I will never let your glory go unnoticed. You are beyond that statue in the Bay of Bengal. You are way beyond the saint that people have been fooled to imagine. You are the Stephen Hawking who has brought me here. I vow that I will bring your work out to the world. She silently prayed with her hands folded.

She presented for exactly 45 minutes, in a state of ecstatic enthusiasm. it was as if Valluvar had possesed her.

There was pin drop silence. After five minutes, the whole lab was on their feet, clapping.

Chaitanya came to her and hugged her saying, "I never knew this was your area of interest. Why are you sitting here and coding software, you should be part of action girl.", she said?

Her friends Meena, Lenka, Bhasker and the whole gang surrounded her and the same old cheer had returned. CHaithanya said she would get an appointment with the director post lunch.

Things suddenly began happening at jet speed. Chaitanya took Selvy to the director, discussed her presentation, the research proposal that could fetch her the Nobel Prize and decided to change her team.

Chaitanya said she would recommend her for the exchange program, to the director. The director immediately called the lab in Germany, since they were closing the appilcations soon. Her exchange was through within minutes. Chaithanya was overjoyed and shared that she would have to leave for Germany in two days.

Selvy was now torn between her dream and her duty to Tamil. She needed to make the choice. She couldn't even muster the courage to tell Chaitanya about her booked tickets, since she had never seen her boss this excited. She went to her room in the evening after her presentation became the talk of the institute.

Selvy casually took her phone. She remembered that she had to crack her *chiththi*'s message.

It read,

53420-31138-38655!

7438-04-02133-0

Ennum ezhuthum...

She knew , this must be Katapayadhi... But her intuition said the message wasn't happy.

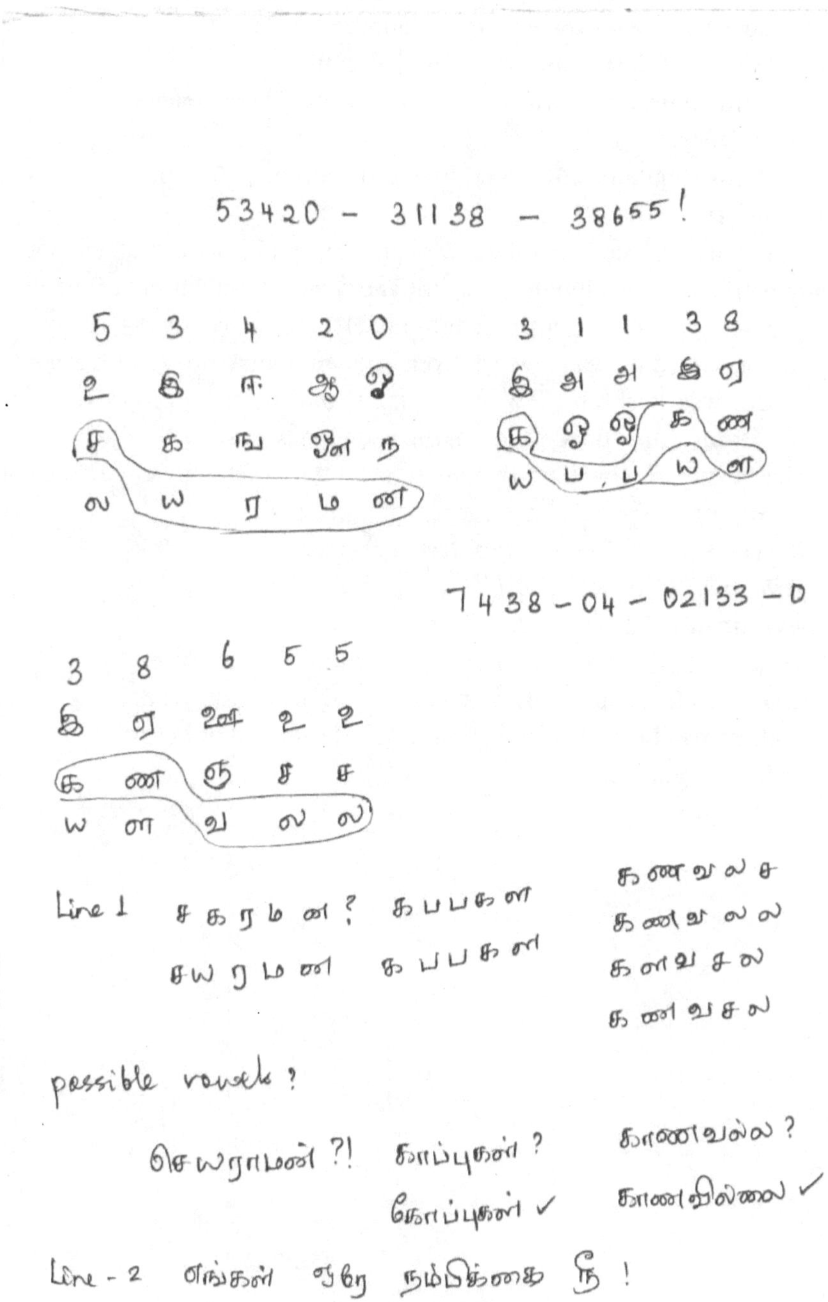

53420 - 31138 - 38655!

7438-04-02133-0

Line 1 ச க ர ம ன ? க ப ப க ள

ச ய ர ம ன க ப ப க ள

க ண வ ல ச

க ண வ ல ல

க ள வ ச ல

க ண வ ச ல

possible vowels ?

செயராமன் ?! காப்புகள் ? காணவல்ல ?

கோப்புகள் ✓ காணவில்லை ✓

Line - 2 எங்கள் ஒரே நம்பிக்கை நீ !

Enter Caption

In the Katapayadhi scheme, every number has 3 letters. we need to use the rules of word formation from Tamil grammar.

1. Words dont begin with certain alphabets. Their vowel combinations should be considered.

2. Words should be attempted first with the consonant in a line and add the appropriate vowel accents.

3. In case a meaningful word cant be made with the consonant combinations, vowels should be taken. The vowels should be added to either the previous or the next consonant to understand the correct word.

So for decoding each word from the numbers, probable consonant sequence was written down and then the most appropriate vowel combinations were added to reveal the coded message.

The beauty of the Katapayadhi scheme was that only a person with knowledge ofthe specific language's logic can decode it.

She cracked the first line and started crying....

*'jeyaraman koppugal kaNavillai'*

Jeyaraman's Files missing.

It was a 20-year penance of Bala *Paati*... and Valli *Chiththi*...

Oh no... in fact something that was due for over 2000 years...

And she had been at the most important crossroad of her life...

To be continued...

CHAPTER THIRTY-FIVE

# Kural chapters and their organization

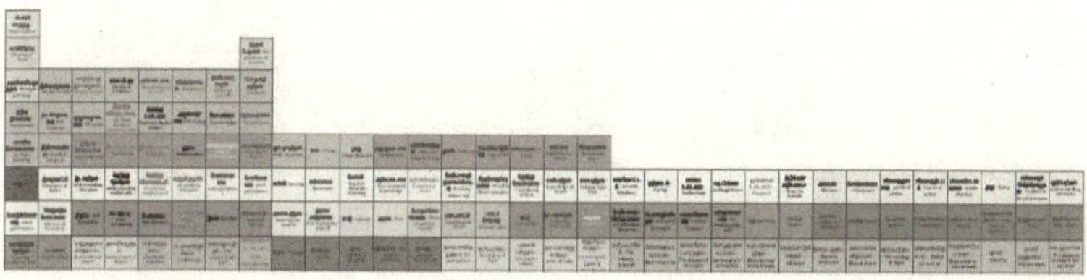

CHAPTER THIRTY-SIX

# Shorthand Notes

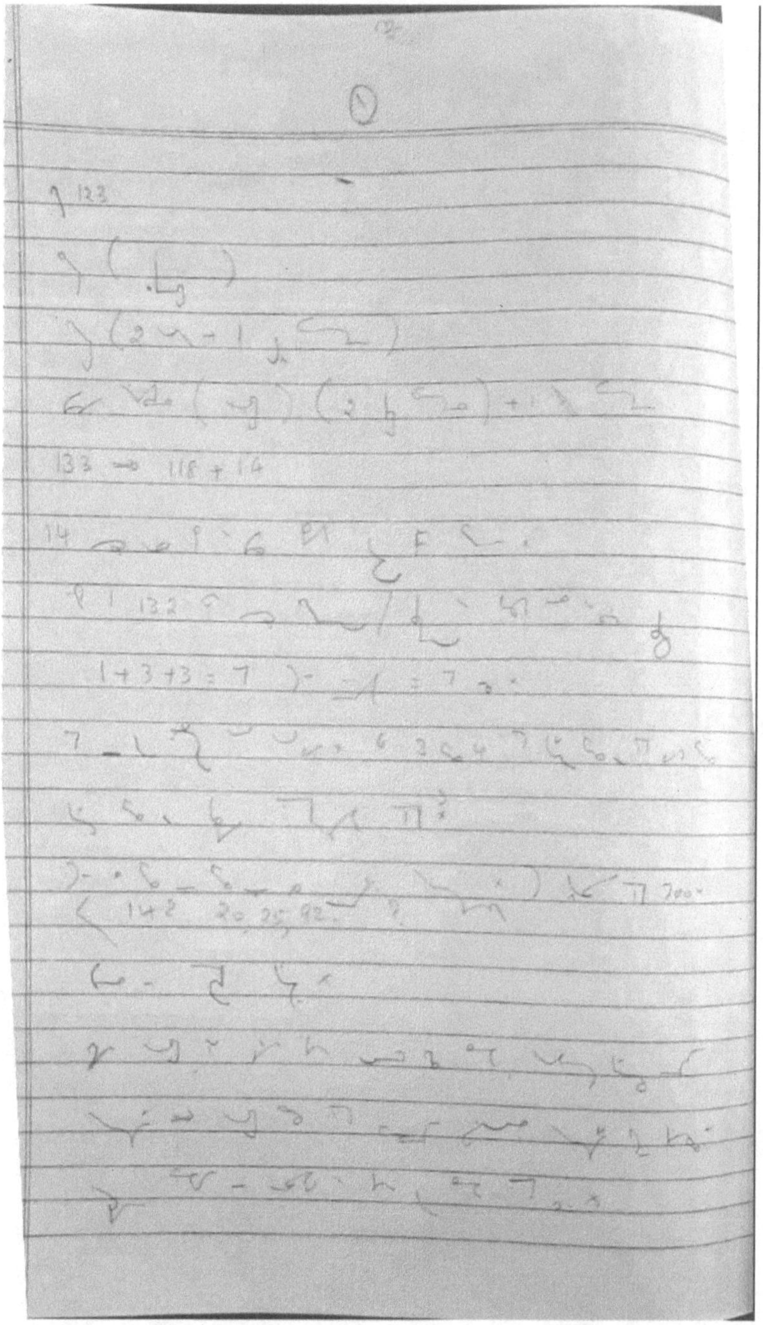

Enter Caption

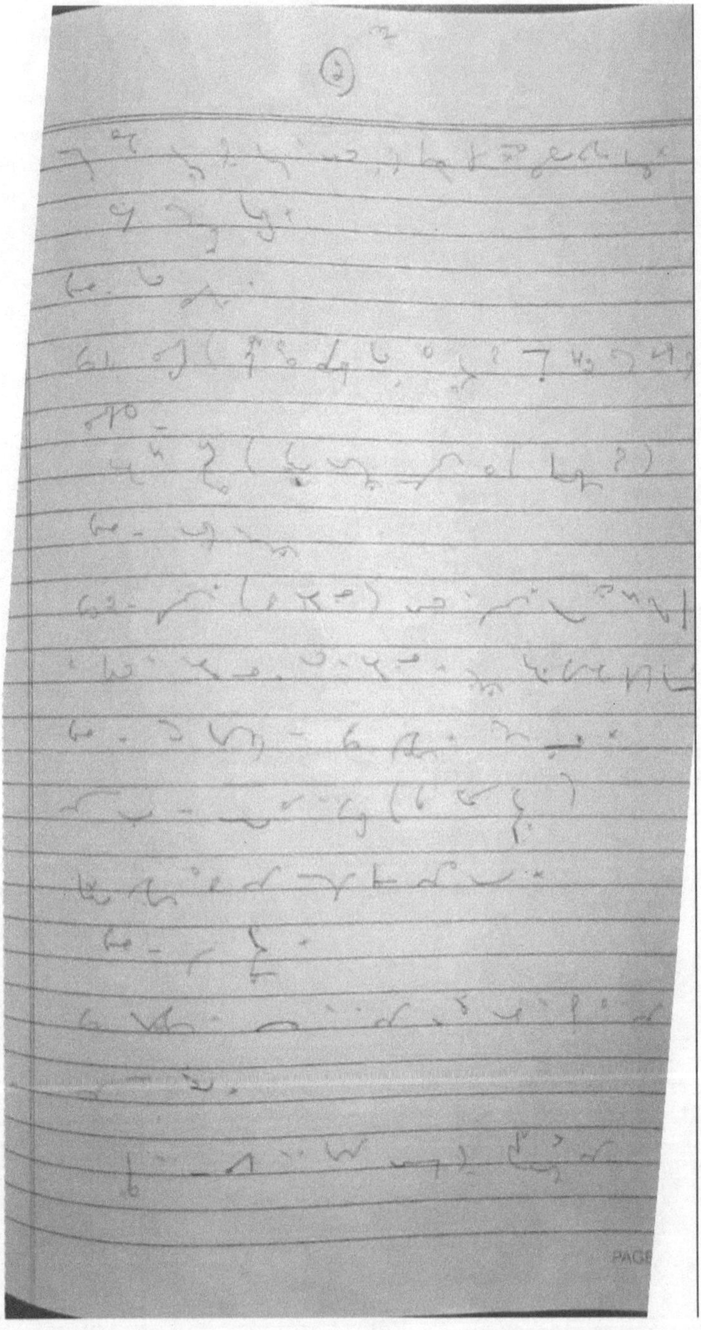

Enter Caption

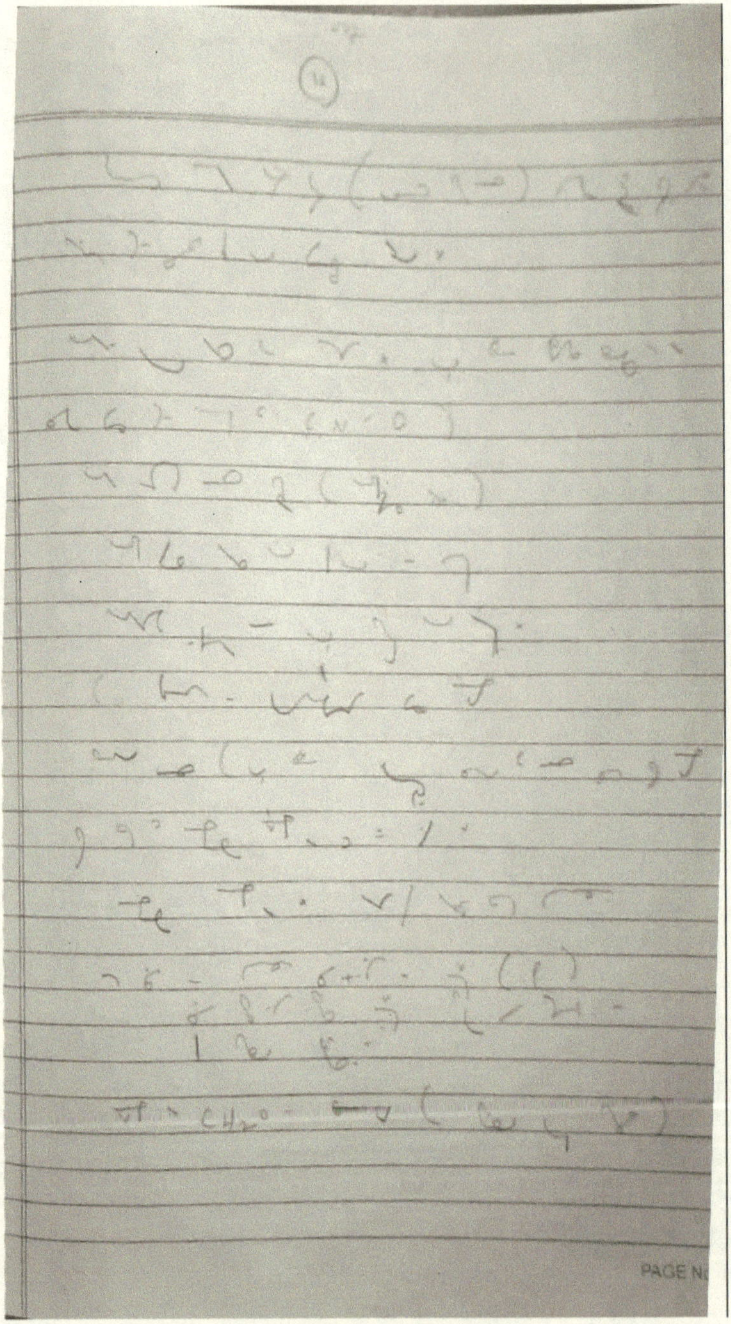

Enter Caption

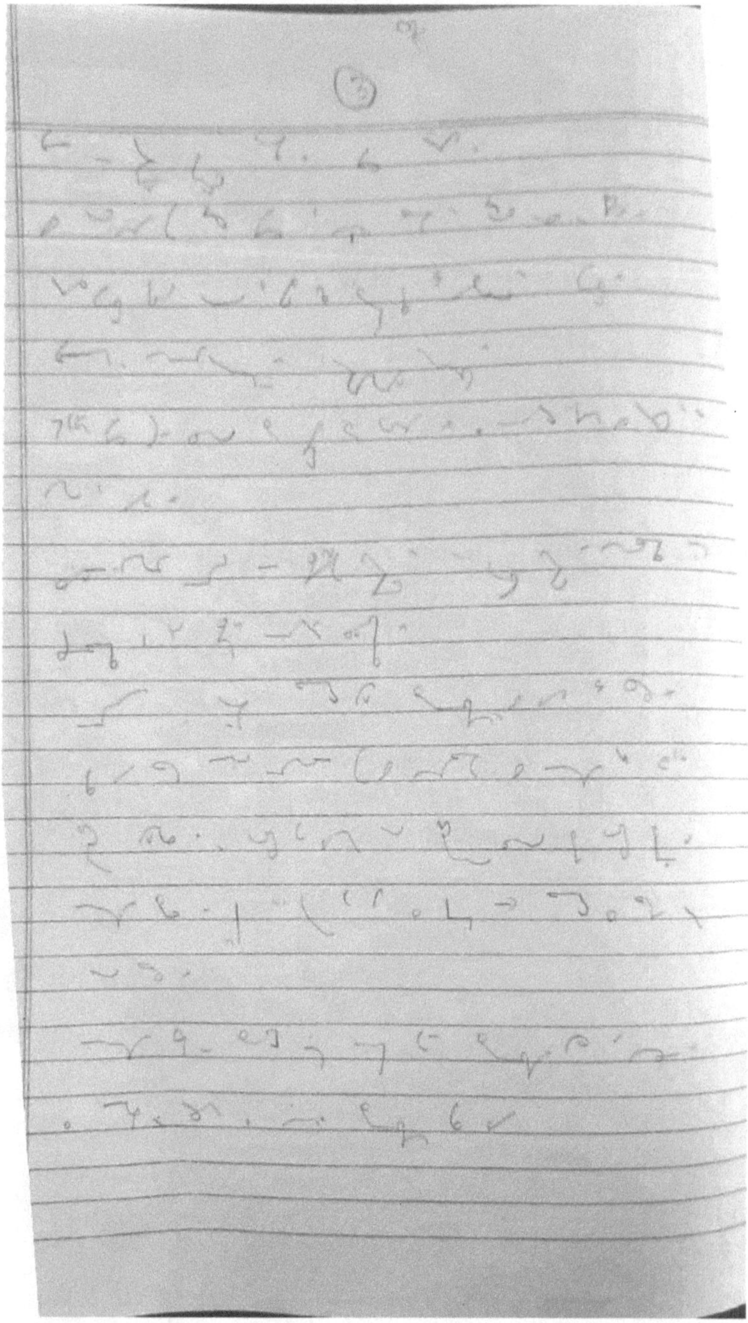

Enter Caption

CHAPTER THIRTY-SEVEN

# Notes

1

அதிகாரம் - 6.

Hydrogen in $\longrightarrow$ $^{12}C + {}^{1}H \longrightarrow {}^{13}N + \gamma$

$^{13}N \longrightarrow {}^{13}C + e^{+} + \nu$

$^{13}C + {}^{1}H \longrightarrow {}^{14}N + \gamma$

$^{14}N + {}^{1}H \longrightarrow {}^{15}O + \gamma$

$^{15}O \longrightarrow {}^{15}N + e^{+} + \nu$

$^{15}N + {}^{1}H \longrightarrow {}^{12}C + {}^{4}He$

↓

Helium out

CNO cycle.

சிருகை அணாஜில் கூடு

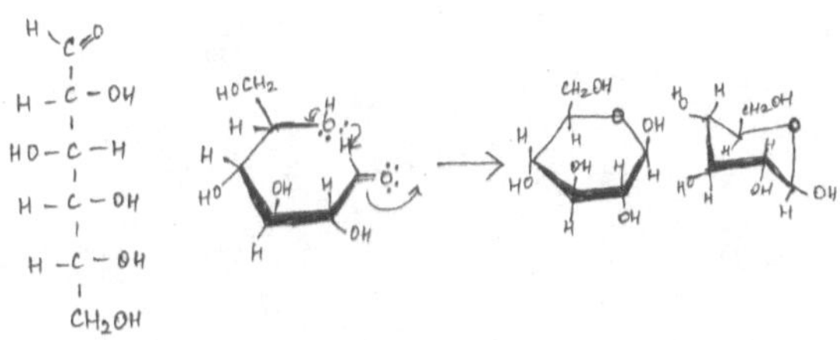

1

அதிகாரம் - 17

Sulphate - +6 - $SO_4^{2-}$

Dithionate - +5 - $S_2O_6^{2-}$

Sulphite - +4 - $SO_3^{2-}$

Disulphite - +4 - $S_2O_5^{2-}$

Dithionate - +3 - $S_2O_4^{2-}$

Thiosulphate - +2 - $S_2O_3^{2-}$

Elemental - 0 - $S^0$

Sulphide - -2 - $S^{2-}$

அதிகாரம் - 18.

| | |
|---|---|
| $HCl$ | -1 |
| $Cl_2$ | 0 |
| $HClO$ | +1 |
| $HClO_2$ | +3 |
| $ClO_2$ | +4 |
| $NaClO_3$ | +5 |
| $NaClO_4$ | +7 |

2

www.ingramcontent.com/pod-product-compliance
Lightning Source LLC
LaVergne TN
LVHW090409210926
848480LV00002B/515
*9798886676464*